SCYTHIA

PROTOSTAR: BOOK ONE OF THE DARK
STELLAR LEGACY

JESSE M HARVEY

Copyright © 2021 Jesse M. Harvey.

All rights reserved. No part of this book may be used or reproduced by any means, graphic, electronic, or mechanical, including photocopying, recording, taping or by any information storage retrieval system without the written permission of the author except in the case of brief quotations embodied in critical articles and reviews.

This is a work of fiction. All the characters, names, incidents, organizations, and dialogue in this novel are either the products of the author's imagination or are used fictitiously.

Books may be ordered through booksellers or at www.jessemharveybooks.com

Because of the dynamic nature of the Internet, any web addresses or links contained in this book may have changed since publication and may no longer be valid. The views expressed in this work are solely those of the author and do not necessarily reflect the views of the publisher, and the publisher hereby disclaims any responsibility for them.

ISBN: 978-1-956344-01-1 (Paperback)

ISBN: 978-1-956344-00-4 (eBook)

Library of Congress Control Number: 1-10816243031

 Created with Vellum

EPIGRAPH

"For my part, I know nothing with any certainty, but the sight of the stars makes me dream." — Vincent Van Gogh

To my Grumpy Wombat, my own light in the darkness.
To my family and friends who helped me start this wonderful journey!
And To those that have joined us.

CONTENTS

PROLOGUE

THE PAIN WAS ALL there was.

There was no end, no beginning.

Just sweet agony searing with icy flames along the capillaries of her soul. She didn't know day or night. There was no time for her.

They ripped away her senses, flooding and consuming her mind with their thoughts. This was the way they broke all those that came before her.

First was the fear of pain. The sheer terror as they were taken from their world to a dark, frightening cell. Then, there was the physical pain. Endless, relentless torture.

If their bodies survived this, that's where he came in.

He was the psychic breaker. He was known for his efficiency. He had broken some of the most difficult psychics. Most were brought in young, before much of the personality was set. But not this one.

She had been born in the void beyond the edge, among the floating stations of dark space. If the missionaries hadn't gone beyond their orders, she might have never been found.

Star-born were not known for being tough; most never made it to this phase. However, she was full grown and had managed to hang on. Even now she resisted.

He had been at her for days with this agony. Burning her memories away. Pulling her thoughts apart. Digging out the little bits she was hiding away.

He had become obsessed. Never had anyone fought so hard to hold on to themselves. The more they struggled, the more it hurt. Most learned the path of least resistance quickly.

She was different; she seemed to ride the agony, using it to hide her true self. She sacrificed meaningless, mundane memories while she hid the moments that meant more. Testing and challenging him in ways he never expected.

Days had gone by as other breakers watched in amazement. No one had ever hung on this long. Never had it taken him so long to break a novice.

All psychics were broken.

All that survive were brought into the order.

Every breaker was broken. It was the cycle. He had been the longest on record. He had lasted eight days before he had lost himself to the pain and given up his mind for peace.

He was exhausted by day five. He had barely eaten. She was given fluids through the tubes in her neck. He had been through her mind many times. He knew her as well as she knew herself; he knew the halls of her mind like the halls of his home.

Every time she fought, he would punish her, but she never stopped fighting. It was almost time; her strength couldn't hold out much longer.

He had taken her father first to remove any sense of

safety he would provide. He would become her new father. He then took her brothers and lovers. He removed all memories of them. There would be no men but him. He had burned and pried her mother away from her, searing away at that maternal bond, trying to find all that remained.

Now she had the fragmented patchwork of her time alone. Those were always the hardest to remove: we cling to our memories with others, but that last true inch of ourselves that makes us unique is the times when we are alone, the moments when no one is watching.

This was the last bit of herself that remained. In the real world he petted her sweaty and bloody face gently. Her skin was a soft, rich blue, and her hair was the deepest orange flame he had ever seen. She was perfection in his mind.

In his fevered delusion, he believed that this pain and connection he had created to break her was like love. At that moment he loved her, as much as he was able to love anything after his own breaking.

She was like the ultimate prize. The perfection. She would be his.

That was how she defeated him.

He reached into her mind and began to pull away her memories of herself.

She knew this was the last of herself. She tucked one small bit of herself buried deep inside the tattered landscape of her mind.

She lured him in with the memory of her first kiss. He had taken the man that had given that kiss, but the feeling of desire remained. She brought it forth like a hot cloud of fog, he reached forward to take it, and she sprung her trap.

She exploded over his mind like molten rock. She pulled forth all the pain and agony she had suffered: days of torture, the fear, pain of loss, and every ounce of the impotent rage she had felt. She gave it to him, all at once.

Flames shot out of his eyes as she held onto his mind, burning him from the inside out. Her fire burned much hotter than his.

Their scream seemed to meld into one voice as the pain crescendoed.

All those who watched quaked with fear, for they didn't just hear that pain with their ears, but every psychic within that cycle felt it.

For her, there was finally an end to the pain.

How she knew that there would be an end, she couldn't tell you.

They had taken too much of her memories. There was only her sense of self and basic understanding of things.

Those that guarded her were afraid to enter the room. The body of her breaker lay a charred mess on the ground. He had been cooked from the inside out. One couldn't even tell if he was a man or not. She yanked his dark robe from his corpse, and smoke billowed from the fortified fabric as she slipped it onto her naked frame.

A voice over a speaker she couldn't see crackled as she rose. "All you have endured is for the Emperor, long live the God-king. You are with us, Scythia."

She tilted her head, listening to the voice. Was it all for the Emperor? The pain, all that agony, was for him?

They didn't know if she was broken. They didn't dare try to find out. Their fear allowed a psychic to be unbroken for the first time in three hundred years.

A little flame danced inside her heart as she stood. Her voice was calm and steady. "For the Emperor," she said, a little giggle bubbling out of her. Oh yes. . . she had something for the Emperor.

She stepped out of that cell with little more than a

whisper. The smoking robes barely shifted as she walked silently down the corridor.

All the other psychics kept their distance. She was like a grenade that hadn't gone off. They had no way of knowing what had transpired during the breaking. It was possible she killed her breaker, though such a thing had never happened before. Not in five hundred years. None were eager to investigate further.

The psychics refused to come within visual range and used the intercom system to direct her from a distance. They called for a shuttle, and guards to escort her to her first assignment. The psychics did not take and easy breath until Scythia had departed.

The shuttles traveled fast, but the news of the Starborn psychic and her bloody breaking was faster than darkness. The fear she had created rippled outward from that moment.

The Ether was alive with the name of her new birth. She knew she would never get back the memories he had taken. She would never remember the faces of those taken.

Her past was empty. Her mind held on only to a few things. But she had her hidden moments. She was comfortable alone in the shuttle. She smiled faintly, closing her eyes and listening to sounds of the world beyond the veil.

The music of the universe. She hummed it as she sat.

Her mind drifted through what few memories remained. The shimmering sparkle of starlight, a pair of red shoes. The sound of her feet running on dark metal corridors of some ship. Hiding under a table listening to someone sing. The feeling of someone brushing her hair.

She had some idea of how to care for herself and even things about the world. They had taken much of her life, but not her intelligence or her cleverness.

"They think I am crazy. . .," she whispered to herself as

her eyes traced the shape of her slender hands and along her delicate fingers. They were long and the same shade of blue as the rest of her. "That my mind is a knotted ball of string. Perhaps they are right; but I am not afraid anymore. I am friends with the monsters. The darkness between the stars is where I live, and the voices in the Ether sing me to sleep. Yes. Think me mad. Think I am crazy. Fear what you can't predict or understand. All the while my fire will burn. That is my plan."

Her laugh was the sound of a beautiful bell ringing out in the back of the shuttle. Its sound jangled with her sharp edges like broken crystal, all sparkles and rainbows from jagged, knife-like pieces.

The two guards who had been assigned to this shuttle said their prayers to the Ancient Undead Gods of Old. These black-hearted soldiers were conditioned to lack fear. However, they did not wish for a slow, painful death.

The tales of horrific deaths at the hands of psychics were the stuff of nightmares. It was a way to keep soldiers in line. Fall in step or we let the psychics have you.

So, the two men swallowed their fear and pretended not to hear the frightening laughter as the shuttle zoomed from the alcove to the conclave. Lord Fallrick was waiting. Once they delivered the psychic, it was up to him as to what to do with her.

They were in agreement that the sooner, the better.

1

WHO THE FUCK IS THAT?

DJAEM WOULD NEVER OPENLY ADMIT that he believed in luck. He had learned that the only fortune he had was that which he made himself. He was born and raised on a hive, an artificially created world made by connecting asteroids and space stations to eventually house over a billion people crowded together in one massive swarm of humanity. One little ant in a colony of billions, he was born to blend in. His face was neither handsome nor ugly, but a bland mix of humanity's features that made him the same as everyone else. With its nice, even tan, brown hair, and brown eyes, his face faded from memory. This was his idea of luck. All his uniqueness was on the inside, in the slums and underground mining tunnels; he learned to read and plan from the minds of the under-world. Djaem was trained from an early age to hide his thoughts and lie with the ease of breathing. It wasn't long before he owned his own block in the hive.

Talent will always rise to the top, they say. However, it does also get you noticed. Djaem knew it could get him in trouble, but he wasn't expecting that it would put him in the position of a sacrifice.

The men with more power than him needed to serve someone up to the imperial forces for certain crimes they didn't want to be investigated. A few of the men knew Djaem could become very powerful if he wanted, so they planned to end him while he was still just a small fish in the ocean of corruption. Djaem almost escaped. His plans within plans left him a number of steps ahead. However, no matter how many tricks you have, one cannot elude one's fate. Despite his best efforts and almost making it to the deep hive, the legion took him off his home world.

The trip was terrifying. The overcrowding on the hive world meant that one was rarely more than a few feet from another person. Even in the deep mines, people were still within visual range. Only in the more expensive places did people have room to be alone. He knew he was being taken to his execution. He decided to face it with as much dignity as he could muster.

He was placed in a room alone, a luxury he had never been able to afford. It became cavernous as he felt himself drifting in the vastness of space. The great open nothing-ness. He felt the loss of his swarm. It was if he lost himself. He was an ant hurled into the air. The cold emptiness filled him, suffocating him. It was worse than death.

When the guards finally came to get him from his room, he almost wept. He was grateful to be taken away. He was looking forward to execution. He would be glad to have it end.

He had no idea how diabolical the Empire truly was until that day.

As he prepared himself for death, they had him change clothes. He was groomed, bathed, and deloused. He was even seen by a physician. He thought perhaps he had to go before some noble before he was executed. As he stood in the inspector general's office, the horrible realization dawned.

His fate was worse than death. He wasn't to be executed.

Death by recruitment, he thought with a grim shudder.

Djaem stood at attention in front of his assigned inspector, listening to his instructions carefully. He was to observe and infiltrate the enemy. He was to interface with the general public and create a smooth operational playing field. His years on the hive would make that simple for him.

He nodded his understanding as the rest of his assigned 'team' entered the office. The brief names and general descriptions he had been given were. . . inadequate.

Uthraith, a mercenary killer from one of the worlds on the outer rings, entered first. He was large and terrible looking. His skin was tattooed extensively in black tribal markings. His body armor was pieced together with skins of monsters he had slain. Skulls of creatures Djaem had no name for hung from his belt in decoration. The skulls were etched and painted with elaborate designs. There seemed to be a competition as to which he had more of, skulls or weapons. His planet was known for its warriors. Its hostile environment and wildlife forced its people to become just as ferocious. They were deadly and efficient, with both primal weapons as well as advanced technology. There were no better hunter-killers in the galaxies.

Strong. Dumb. Very dangerous. A beast. His mind processed the information, then adjusted and swirled with new calculations.

Following in the wake of this murder-mountain walked a woman. Raza was smaller, pretty, and deadly, like a spider.

Her dark hair was swept up off her neck and coiled in an elaborate braid at the back of her head. Her pale skin helped draw attention to her bright green eyes and full mouth. She was graceful, and her big eyes gave her an innocent face, but Djaem knew a killer when he saw one. She was a 'sneak' like him. Djaem specialized in manipulation and planning. They were both walking lies, but he could see that she was more about the quick cons, fast heists, or silent kills.

Handler for the beast. She'll be a useful tool, but I must be sure she's not using me back. His mind contemplated her carefully, assessing and weighing her threat and value.

She seemed to nod her understanding to him in the silent speech. It confirmed what he already knew. Only those in his profession knew this secret language. A careful display of communication in body postures and hand gestures was shared among those that needed to be in the know.

"I know you understand. I am his handler. Don't worry, you have a different job," she communicated in the silent speech, and he acknowledged but gave nothing away.

She smiled at the inspector as the mercenary took up an intimidating posture a few feet away. Raza the spider busied herself looking over the handheld data screen given to her by the inspector.

"Fallrick, what is with these files? I know better than to expect much from the data center, but this is just plain incompetence. There are a dozen birth records for this hiver, and none for the psychic." The spider woman looked exasperated as she scrolled through the files. "They have his age ranging from fifteen to thirty-five." Her green eyes went back to Djaem, studying him as she looked between him and the pictures.

Inspector Fallrick gave a little laugh. "Apparently the

face recognition computers had a hard time with him. It may have been why it was so hard to track him on the hive. I think that will be a great advantage to us." His smile was full of practiced patience and tolerance.

Djaem was aware of the veiled threats and double-talk they were sharing. She had already established a rapport with the man. He was in a position of authority, and she was looking to increase her station.

"Fine, I guess it doesn't matter now that we have him. But you know how I feel about working with children." She glared, tossing the data screen down on the desk. Djaem looked over and scanned the information there as the spider continued expressing her displeasure.

Fallrick's face lost a little of its pleasantness. "There are no children on this team."

Raza's eyes narrowed as her lips flattened. "There are no birth records, but it says here the psychic completed her induction forty-eight hours ago, no finishing school. That means a kid."

Fallrick stood up to meet her gaze head-on. "I assure you; she is a special case. We may not know how old she is, but you know I don't use children for these teams."

The spider glared, and in that space between moments, Djaem tested the waters. "She is a year older than me." He mused easily as if he had been a part of this discussion the whole time.

The spider's green eyes snapped back to him as if she were seeing him for the first time. "How would you even know that?" She crossed her arms, waiting imperiously for his answer.

Djaem kept his smile to himself as he motioned to the data screen. "Look at the screen. The Star-weaver incident happened nineteen years ago. If she was really born during that, it makes her nineteen, one year older than me."

Uthraith laughed loudly from the corner. "Little pair of younglings. It has been that many cycles since I was that age, and half as many for you." He grinned at Raza. She rolled her eyes and shook her head at Uthraith.

"Oh, shut up old man."

She was ambitious. Djaem didn't like that. Ambition was dangerous. He wanted to find himself a corner of the world and keep it. This silly woman had no idea the death she was seeking.

This will be easy. She loves control. Give her the illusion of it, his mind assured him.

There was a strange sound from out in the hall. The beast shifted his stance as his instincts told him danger approached. Djaem felt all the hairs on his neck stand on end. Everyone turned to watch the door. The air was charged before the door shifted open, and a guard walked in quickly, stepping to the side to allow the next person to follow him.

Djaem's breath stopped for a moment. His mind froze, his heart tripped slightly in his chest. He had never seen a Star-born before. She was tall, over six feet. Much taller than Djaem's five feet eight. Her skin was a shade of blue he had never seen, soft and faded but impossibly clear. Her hair was living fire: shades of red and orange mixing with highlights of white and yellow. Her eyes were black bottomless irises in pale whites. Her lips were a soft shade of orange, matching the hair on her head. She was both terrifying and breathtaking.

She was wearing a strange, ill-fitting robe that looked like it had been set on fire. It appeared she wore nothing else. Her feet were bare and filthy. Her hair was wild and went in every direction like it hadn't been washed or combed in days. Honestly, she looked like a prisoner who had gotten loose. She walked fully into the room past the guard who had preceded her. The guard was to one side, allowed her to pass, and kept his eyes carefully away from her.

Where is his pair? Guards are supposed to work in doubles, Djaem's mind whispered.

The guard had seemed rock steady until he spoke. Djaem heard the terror in his voice as he announced his charge.

"Scythia. . . level alpha psychic, grade initiate." His voice cracked. "Fresh from the training sector, delivered as ordered." He managed to get the last out. The guard was grateful for his helmet. No one could see him sweat.

Inspector Fallrick remained calm as he looked her over. "You may depart," he said. The guard fled the room.

She watches no one and expects nothing? Djaem's mind questioned carefully.

She barely spared a glance to anyone as she came into the lavish room. Her dirty bare feet didn't make a sound against the carpet floor; but she was distracted by them. Djaem realized quickly she was feeling the floor with her toes like a child. Curling and uncurling them in thick plushness.

Her dark eyes moved to them all in turn, taking in their reactions to her presence, almost mirroring these reactions back. The beast leered at her half-naked form, and the spider woman looked at her with both disdain and caution. Djaem made sure to smile at her. She walked to the inspector when he beckoned her like one would a child. He plucked a brightly colored candy from the crystal bowl on his desk.

"Here you are, dear. Scythia, is it? Here, you have this.

It's a sweetie, you will like it." Fallrick said in his overly friendly voice.

She didn't like that. She hides it well, Djaem's mind observed, spotting the tiny tells that only he seemed to perceive.

She took the candy, and after some prompting, put it in her mouth. Her eyes went wide as her face broke out in joy. She moved closer to the inspector. He held out a bowl and patted her head. She allowed him as she quietly examined the brightly colored candies.

Djaem managed to keep from fidgeting but only just. *What is she? This isn't right.* His mind whirled, trying to calculate her threat and being unable to quantify her.

The beast tilted his head to get a better look at the blue skin that was showing in the holes of the robe. This seemed to prompt a bit of jealousy in the spider woman, who pushed his enormous shoulder, her eyes sharp.

"What's wrong with her?" asked Raza, leaning forward to sniff her. "She smells like charred meat." She made a disgusted face and dismissed her. "Is she stupid?"

The blue woman, Scythia, froze. Her dark eyes shifted towards Raza; her mouth filled with candy till her cheeks bulged. Scythia tilted her head to one side in a curious, almost catlike motion. Even with all his foresight, Djaem had only enough time to tense before it happened.

Raza suddenly gasped in agony and fell to the floor. She writhed in a pain so intense her scream couldn't escape. The beast moved with lightning reflexes, faster than Djaem could see.

He almost reached Scythia. He almost had his deadly grasp around her delicate, blue throat. It would have taken less than a heartbeat to end her.

Almost was not enough.

His massive hand grasped at the empty air in front of

her as he collapsed at her feet with a loud thud. His jaws clenched, and the sound of his grinding teeth filled the room. He jerked and twitched. All his size and power reduced to quivering jelly on the floor.

She looked at them with feline curiosity, her head tilting to one side, then the other, slowly studying them as she finished the candy in her mouth. She then looked at the inspector, who had stepped back. Scythia placed a bright red candy in her mouth.

She's no ordinary psychic. . . She's, my death. Djaem's mind came to its conclusion.

She spoke softly at first, as if unsure what the words would sound like. "I am not stupid," she said slowly but firmly. Turning around, she spotted Djaem, who had remained still and silent.

He felt his insides freeze in terror as he looked at those bottomless eyes, but he kept his smile in place, terror making words escape the prison of his throat. His instincts took over his speech.

"You are not stupid; anyone can see that. It's just. . . that outfit simply doesn't suit you. Raza didn't mean to offend you; she just speaks without thinking sometimes," he said to her quickly, keeping his hands still so that he was nonthreatening.

She blinked those dark eyes at him. She studied him carefully before she took a step towards him. The other people in the room gasped out in unison as she released whatever power she had been using to hurt them. The spider woman staggered to her feet and moved to lean against the beast who had barely risen to his knees. He made some ward against evil with his hand. Those from the feral worlds were superstitious and didn't like psychics. They had good reason.

The spider woman glared at the inspector. "What the

hell, Fallrick, you said we were getting the strongest psychic, not some double-crossing whack job." She practically spat the words in a heated whisper. The inspector was smiling as he sat down in his chair with a thump.

The strongest? . . . I don't see it. This group wouldn't be given the most powerful anything. Djaem inwardly shook his head.

Fallrick just smiled. "She is magnificent," he whispered softly. "There are suppressors in this room. Most psychics couldn't even think too loud in here. But she acts as if it were no more trouble than the buzzing of flies."

Scythia reached out and touched Djaem's hair. He remained still; some part of him was grateful for the touch. There was too much space in this room. She slipped her blue fingers through the soft curls without a thought of personal space. After petting him gently, she lifted a candy to his lips, pushing it into his mouth with great attention. Of course, he allowed her to do as she pleased with him, considering her display of power. He vaguely hoped that the candies were not laced with something.

Djaem kept his fear in check as this strange, frightening creature grabbed his wrist and lifted his hand to her own head. She moved his hand to pet her disheveled and dirty hair. Her hands were surprisingly warm, which seemed disjointed with her blue skin. She began forcing Djaem to feed her the candies and pat her head like the inspector had done. Djaem began to relax and followed her cues easily. She was like a child testing the boundaries and figuring out how everything works, including who gave her candy and who didn't, who she liked and who she didn't.

Calm begets calm, Djaem. Keep cool.

He began to entertain her the way he did countless children back home, with a shiny coin and magic tricks. Her eyes widened in delight at his sleight of hand.

"Why is she so childlike?" he asked the inspector as she tried to find the coin he had made disappear in his pocket.

Another voice answered from the door. The entire room had missed his entrance.

"She is defective. She didn't complete the training. They got through her mind wipe, but that's as far as they went." The new man's insignia marked him as Special Division. They oversaw training and breaking psychics. It also meant he was a psychic himself.

Djaem watched Scythia as her expression changed and anger flared in her eyes. Suddenly that innocent curiosity was gone, replaced by dangerous calculations. Fear ran a finger down Djaem's back as those dark eyes turned towards the Special Division.

2

WHAT THE FUCK DID YOU JUST DO?

SPECIAL DIVISION LUCIAS was higher ranking than Inspector Fallrick behind the desk. The two men were assigned to different departments, which allowed for rivalry without outright confrontation. The 'head cases,' as the hivers called psychics back home, had a weird ranking system that had always sounded creepily religious to Djaem. He knew there was more between these men than rank, but that would take time to discover.

The woman, Scythia, turned to look at the Special Division Officer. Her body was relaxed as she examined him. Her lithe frame stretched above him by half a head. Lucias managed to look down his nose at her even then. The disdain was clear. She continued to stare at him quite serenely, patiently.

Djaem understood who the officer was almost instantly. He was everything Djaem wasn't tall, handsome, muscular, and polished, almost regal. His display of arrogance was impressive. He was a man that got what he wanted, one way or another. He was made of pride and spite, driven by ambition and power. The only question that lingered in Djaem's mind was *Is he foolish?*

The officer barely gave Scythia a second glance. He was here to posture, to put the fear of psychics into the team. He dismissed the mad psychic, confident in his own status and strength. He was here to undercut a rival, not bother with a broken tool.

Djaem watched the interaction between the two leaders with interest. The Special Division Officer was playing a deadly game with the inspector, and this was all part of that competition. These were the machinations that men in the middle had to play to rise in rank.

Djaem knew what they would do. The officer would make some veiled threats and some not so veiled ones. The inspector would be forced to cow down to his superior in front of the new subordinates, and therefore the pecking order would be established. The inspector would make some carefully worded statement to show his defiance and create an 'us versus them' dynamic to help bring the team together. Everyone would fall in line and know their place. This was how these games were played.

Djaem had already watched it all play out in his head. He calculated that the reason both he and Miss Ambitious Spider were here was because the inspector wanted to beat his rival and move up the food chain. Djaem's mind was spinning ahead, moving the pieces around in his mental chessboard. He glanced at the tall, blue woman as he tried to make his plans. She was throwing off his calculations. *What was she to this scheme?*

Djaem had been half-listening to the speeches while his mind formulated plans when some of the words began to sink past his thoughts.

"Her breaker died during the training, losing all her memories to the Ether. The trainers say she has brain damage. Giving her to you was of no consequence to us. If you want to pick up the refuse, who am I to deny you? What use is a mindless psychic to me? But I guess she is a Star-born, and pretty. Maybe she has some uses to you. . .," the officer sneered with disgust, looking between the women in the room and Fallrick. Raza and Uthraith had obviously seen this dance before and were standing impassively, pretending they were deaf. Behind the mask of a pleasant smile, Fallrick's jaw clenched, muscles twitching.

Djaem looked at the tall woman; her mind seemed somewhere else. She was humming a strange little tune. Suddenly, Scythia started to giggle. The sound terrified him.

Her voice was soft and almost sultry as she spoke. "I wonder." She looked at Officer Lucias. He frowned at her interruption as she pointed a long, delicate blue finger at him, and in a sexy, breathless whisper, uttered, "Pain."

Division Officer Lucias, one of the most experienced psychics in the sector, was completely unprepared for her mental assault. His natural resistance, along with the suppressors in the room, should have made such an attack completely impossible. This was not the first time a psychic had resisted him, and usually it's nothing more than a scratch against his mental armor. Normally he would let them try. He would allow them to crash upon his defenses like waves on rocks. Then he would put them in their place. Her mind was completely different, not scratching at his armor, but hitting him with lightning from the void. First there was nothing, and then suddenly there was nothing but pain. He cried out in surprise and anger as he crumpled to the floor. Screaming in agony, he curled inward trying to protect himself; he failed.

Sparks flew from the tiny boxes next to each light fixture. Completely overwhelmed, the psychic suppressors blew. The auto-extinguishers kicked on to put out the small fires started by the rain of sparks.

"Oh, things can feel pain too," the blue woman said, amazed in childlike wonder.

With that single moment, all of Djaem's calculations were ruined. He scrapped them all. A weapon, that's what she was, a doomsday device with a broken safety. For a moment Djaem marveled in both awe and horror at the possibilities this woman added to the future. Djaem looked at the inspector, who stood there with shock and pleasure in equal measure on his face. The man had been looking for a tool, but he was as surprised as the rest of them. Djaem felt himself relax a bit. That meant he hadn't planned this. He had simply been casting a wide net.

Scythia laughed in childlike glee, smiling proudly at her handiwork. "In the Name of the Emperor," she said in a sing-song voice. She continued to giggle as she popped another candy in her mouth. It was the slogan for the Special Division. They were part of the private police for the Emperor's Nationalist Enforcement Bureau. Technically, everyone in this room was part of the N.E.B. The big difference was that the Special Division also enforced universal laws. An enforcer within the enforcement.

An officer within the Special Division was supposed to be so much more powerful than rank-and-file psychics like her. However, there he was, crumbled at her feet, writhing in agony.

Djaem knew this would get out of hand quickly and needed to be deescalated. He reached out and gently placed a hand on her shoulder. He kept his voice sweet and pleasant. "Miss Scythia, excellent job. . . Please. . . He is making quite a bit of noise. Could you stop now? You made your point. You're very clever."

She blinked at Djaem for a moment and sighed. The

man stopped screaming and gasped for breath. She watched him with abject curiosity, as if this were the most important part of her experiment. The officer slowly rose to his feet with as much dignity as he could muster. He brushed off his uniform and straightened his collar. Somehow, he regained his composure, and though the arrogance was gone, his pride remained.

"You should be careful, Fallrick, this new dog of yours needs to learn when to growl and when to bite." He looked at her directly with respect warring with jealousy on his face. "You caught me off guard. It won't happen again, Scythia," he said before turning and walking out.

Of all the scenarios Djaem had imagined, the officer Scythia had just assaulted and sent to the ground walking out as if nothing had happened was not high on the list. Neither was the blatant satisfaction on Fallrick's face.

Scythia relaxed and smiled contentedly as she looked around the room and then back to Djaem.

The beast laughed as he maneuvered his massive frame into a seat, his head still higher than most in the room. "I think she will do, Raza," he spoke to the spider woman. "She has no fear at all. She may be a witch, but at least she spreads the pain out evenly."

Raza rolled her eyes as she sighed. "Yeah. . . I suppose it was fun watching that pompous ass squirm like the maggot he is. However, I didn't expect him to just leave. That man is made of pure spite. He will want revenge. We need to be careful."

Raza leaned her hip against the edge of Fallrick's desk, folding her arms. Her elegantly painted face pulled into a frown as she looked at Djaem. "Why didn't she use her power on you?"

Djaem shrugged, feigning dumb. "How would I know that?"

Raza straightened and moved towards Djaem and Scythia. "Well, she seems to like you. Maybe because your face is so simple. Like those dolls they give to babies to put them at ease."

Djaem nodded as he considered the theory. He prided himself on his bland, forgettable appearance. "That sounds possible, actually," he agreed without any resentment.

Raza smiled, a gleam in her dark eyes. "She will be valuable if she is as powerful as she seems, as long as we can train her."

Victory was the one unspoken word in Djaem's mind. *Victory.*

Fallrick leaned forward on his desk as his smile crawled across his face. "Yes, she is marvelous. But we really should do something about her clothes. She looks like an escapee." He said softly and passed out data crystals to each of them. They glowed with the ambient light in the room. "Those are your assignments and orders. It will tell you where your dorm is and your account information. Djaem, I am putting you in charge of making sure Scythia gets all the help she needs to integrate into the society around her. Get her some lessons, clothes, and make sure she can read all those things. Your first mission leaves in two days." That disturbing smile never left his face. Raza motioned to Uthraith, who rose easily and led the way out the door.

Djaem tried not to wince outwardly as he thought about his job. He was going to have to work overtime as her handler. Miss Spider didn't yet realize she had been passed up for promotion. Overseeing the most dangerous weapon in Fallrick's arsenal was quite the position for the new guy. Though technically, it seemed that this weapon had picked her own handler.

Djaem followed along behind the tall woman, making

sure that she stayed with the group. She seemed to have no problem keeping up with the group. She smiled happily as she ate one small candy after another as they left the office.

Fallrick sat back, returning to his documents as his new minions filed out. He didn't bother asking for his candy dish back.

Djaem walked with the group quietly down the long hallway. The beast and the spider were already plotting as they approached the elevators. When they reached the doors, Djaem noticed that one of the guards took a small step away from Scythia. The other remained stone still, but the brim of his hat trembled. The shaking brim gave him away even as he kept his eyes forward. Both men were pale and avoided looking in her direction.

Djaem frowned as the realization dawned. Scythia had practiced her little game of pain before she even reached the office. She glanced at Djaem and gave him a mischievous wink. *So, she's only pretending not to see their fear.* The beast was used to being the object of fear, so he barely registered it, and his little companion gave no sign of noticing either. It was very hard to calculate how much Scythia actually understood about what was happening around her. In the quiet elevator she began to hum that strange little tune again as her eyes rolled back in her head. She was listening to something only she could hear.

Raza shook her head, eyeing Scythia. "Little nutter. We really need to do something about her. I don't want people to see her like this and think this is how our team works."

Uthraith just shrugged and looked at Scythia again. "She looks like she has just come from a rowdy bed," he grinned and rolled his shoulders as he chuckled. "Women look good this way."

Raza rolled her eyes and shook her head. "You would say that about any women."

Uthraith smiled, unapologetic. "Yes. All women are good, all shape, all size. I like."

Djaem became aware of the atmosphere between those two. *Ahh. Seduction. That's the leash you keep him on. It keeps you physically close and makes them easier to watch. Emotional closeness keeps you safe. Good choice, little spider. It's one of the best choices as a handler. Even if there's no sex in it, once you build the connection, you build the control.*

He thought again how the rest of 'his' team had looked piled up in agony. He carefully considered how to proceed as they headed to the electric transport that would shuttle them to their dormitory. *I'd rather be the one seducing him than even consider it with her. If anything went wrong. . .* Djaem shuddered at the idea.

Djaem took his terrifying blue charge to her room, where she began to wander about. "You should get cleaned up. Do you know how to work the shower?"

Raza walked in behind them. "I will help her. I don't want her to embarrass us. So, I will get her clean. . . Just get her something to wear. This is completely ruined. Not to mention it was made for someone shorter than her and. . . male." Raza looked at the garment in confusion and then disgust as she sniffed at it. She shooed Scythia towards the bathroom.

Djaem nodded and smiled a little at the worried blue face, which was looking at him seriously. "Listen to Raza. You will feel better after being clean. No hurting anyone until I get back, ok?" he said, trying to keep his voice even and calm. *Until I get back. . . that's like an invitation to make me her next target,* he mused to himself.

Scythia followed Raza towards a back room. He walked out, his mind stumbling to make the new piece fit as he left the womenfolk alone. None of this lined up with anything he had experienced before. He should have been executed by now. Perhaps he still would be. Perhaps he was someone else's plan, someone else's piece to be sacrificed to further their game.

SCYTHIA SANK into the warmth of a bubble bath. She ignored the voice that was talking. Her entire focus was on the feel of warm water against her skin and bristles scrubbing her clean. She watched the bubbles float around her. Up and down, up and down, she poked her toes through the surface of the hot water.

So many sensations, they were both new and nostalgic. Some part of her knew that she should remember this. That this was not the first time she had felt these things. However, her mind had no access to those memories. She chose not to concern herself with what she didn't know. Instead, she focused on making new memories.

Lifting the rainbow bubbles up, she blew them off her fingertips.

She followed Raza's instructions and washed her hair. She shifted and grumbled as the other woman ran a brush through the tangles and snarls of the wet orange mess, trying to get it into some semblance of order. By the time she was clean, Raza was soaked.

After she was scrubbed, her skin felt light and was a radiant, glowing blue. Scythia stepped out of the bathing chamber into the sleeping area. She paused to look at the clothes laid out on the bed. She managed to figure out how to wear the outfit. She tilted her head as she looked at herself in the reflective glass. *It seems a little pointless to wear,* she mused to herself as she considered the front and back. The fabric was shimmering and pretty but scratchy and rough on her skin. It was like the robe she had earlier but almost sheer white. It gathered at her shoulders, and where there should have been sleeves, it hung open in wide gaps down to her hips. There was a wide opening at her neck down to draping open almost to her navel. The material gathered again at her waist cinched slightly and hung down to her ankles in the front and back. The sides again gapped open as if whole pieces were missing. *Perhaps I put it on wrong.* Finally, she stepped out of the sleeping room. Raza and the large man with the markings on his face stood watching her. These clothes were loose and light. They did nothing to keep the cold away.

The enormous man had a strange expression on his face as he looked her up and down for a moment. Scythia didn't like it and thought about inflicting pain on him again, but Djaem had said not to till he arrived. Raza had the good sense to have Uthraith leave the room.

Scythia looked around for food as she was getting very hungry.

When Djaem finally arrived back with not just clothes but a plate with something that smelled delicious on it, she was very happy. Her stomach growled in response. He frowned as he looked at her clothes.

"Who gave you this?" he said quietly. She watched his face; it changed color slightly at his neck. His voice had a soothing quality that felt nice against her ear. She liked it when he spoke. She nodded towards Raza as she put a piece of whatever was on the plate in her mouth. It was warm and juicy and made her want to eat more. He sighed and rubbed a spot on his forehead. "Don't wear this in front of people. This is for private wearing. It shows too much skin."

Curiosity plagued her as she ate. "Skin is bad?" she mumbled around the food.

He shook his head, his face in a smile, but she saw his

emotions in the Ether. He was worried and frustrated. His expressions were a face but not a real face. It was a transparent sheen encompassing his mind. His thoughts were a wonder, a dazzling display for her to behold. She could watch him think for hours. His mind was a crystal palace made of prismatic puzzles, shifting and moving around as he planned.

"No. It does, however, leave you exposed, and others will look at you in ways you may not like. Is it comfortable to wear?" he asked, curiosity coloring his Ether as the light inside pulsed.

She shook her head, wrinkling her nose. "No, it's cold. And it scratches in weird places." She considered the outfit again. "If I am going to be this cold, I would rather not wear anything." He gave a laugh and smiled. This time she could see the humor in his Ether. It helped warm the color. She felt herself smile in return.

"Let's try some of these things on. You tell me what you like best, ok?" he said as he motioned to the bags, he'd brought with him.

She finished eating the food on the plate and followed him. He took her back to the sleeping room to change. It seemed more trouble than it was worth—all the putting things on, moving around, and taking them off—but she could tell Djaem thought it was important, so she did what he asked.

Seeing his lights and colors helped her figure out what he wanted from her. She could see the others' lights, but they weren't as bright or as clear as Djaem's. Her Djaem was special. He was her guiding light.

Eventually, she found some she liked. A soft silky top that fit under the uniform jacket, and a long skirt that was made of a stiffer but silky material, which made a wonderful swishing sound when she moved. It flowed around her legs and lifted when she spun in a circle. She grinned and spun again, swishing it around herself, back and forth.

The feel and sound helped blot out the constant hum from the Ether. That hum was always close, like music behind a thick current. Each person had a sound, a shine; it all blurred together in the Ether, forming beautiful music and lights. It was hard for Scythia to be two places at once. She was dancing between the Here and now, and there and then. The feel of the fabric seemed to bring her more firmly to Here, providing a shield from the There.

Djaem was smiling as she swished around. She liked it when he smiled. It made his lights bright and his hum pleasant. "The fabric is called silk. It's organic. Supposedly the natural fibers will help you focus and protect against the Ether." He pulled out a pair of slippers, also made of silk. It was all a matching dark black with silver sparkles and beads sewn on and just the faintest hint of red at the edges. She loved them and kept swishing around. Her smile stretching across her face.

RAZA WHISTLED LOW from the door. "Against her blue skin and fiery hair, she cuts a striking figure. I washed her hair and braided it around to one side. It's in fashion of late. Now she could pass for nobility with her high cheekbones and strong chin. She is a beautiful woman." Raza gave a critique as she moved around Scythia.

Djaem nodded as he continued to watch Scythia swish around the room. She reminded him of stories that his grandmother told about the goddess worshiped by the people from beyond the rim. She was beautiful and dangerous, full of wonder and fury. Chaos.

The outer edges of the Empire were riddled with colonies that have evolved differently than the rest of the Empire. Some of the people were barely recognizable as human. This helped keep many people from traveling to the far reaches. Star-born were people who lived their whole life in space.

This Star-born was easy to read, but the book was dangerous. *Best to tread lightly*, he thought. "Now Scythia, you understand that you are supposed to listen to me, right?" he asked gently, making sure her eyes were focused on him.

She nodded and smiled. "I am supposed to listen to Djaem and follow his instructions." She tried to look reassuring to him. "I will do my best. Djaem is special."

Djaem frowned slightly. When was the last time someone called him that? "Okay. Well, it's very important that we work together, and you follow my instructions. I will try to anticipate things you will need to know. You can listen to Raza and Uthraith, but I am more important to listen to, ok? Trust me."

Scythia was nodding along with his words and then blinked. "Trust. Trust you?" Djaem stopped as he realized what he was asking and sighed. "Yes. Scythia, this will only work if we trust each other. You trust me to tell you what to do and that it will be what is best. And I will trust you to do it and to make sure you don't do anything to hurt me."

She tilted her head and nodded. "Make sure I don't hurt you. Should I stop other people from hurting you?" She watched him intently, and he could see her curiosity and her eagerness. Djaem sighed in relief. "Yes. That would be nice. I don't like being hurt. Also, I will try and make sure no one tricks you or lies to you."

She nodded. "Partners," she said, holding out a hand.

He blinked in surprise and shook her hand. "Partners. Where did you learn that?"

She smiled and whispered, "From the Ether. It is floating around me, whispering and singing." She motioned around the room to things he couldn't see or hear.

Raza shook her head. "We call that 'touched' where I come from. Don't strain her too much, Djaem. It's not worth breaking her brain just to teach her a few niceties. She is our big gun; we don't need her to be polite." She grinned malevolently. Raza continued as she nodded her approval. "We teach her to be intimidating and strike fear in our enemies. Fear is the currency of the Empire, and she makes us rich. Look at her, the way she moves, her coloring. She will be like a poster child for Fallrick and us."

Djaem watched his dangerous weapon, who was currently humming and swishing her skirt back and forth. "We can work up to that. Even if she is a little off, we need to make sure we are all working together."

Scythia smiled brightly and leaned in to whisper into Djaem's ear. In a voice only his mind heard, she said, "Don't worry, Djaem. You all think I'm crazy. . . But that's my plan."

A shiver ran along Djaem's body again as a new feeling came with her whisper. She wasn't kidding. She may be crazy, but she wasn't as helpless as she seemed. He saw her eyes sparkle with mirth. *Plague upon plagues! She knows exactly how dangerous she is!*

3

DAY OF DEPARTURE FOR
MISSION ONE

DJAEM TOOK his seat next to Scythia on the launch shuttle. It was different from the transport that had brought him here. That had been a prisoner-vessel, and he had been in a cell. This was the small shuttle that would take them to the larger orbital-transport ship. He didn't know what to expect as he checked his buckle one more time.

Raza and Uthraith sat a few seats away; they managed to look both bored and intimidating at once. In this world, it was a basic skill set for anyone in a position of authority.

Djaem looked over at Scythia, who was grinning excitedly; her eyes wide, she kept looking out the window. She bounced like a child in her seat. She pulled against the straps he had just buckled for her. She looked like the little boy three rows over with his family. In fact, they had begun making faces at each other, giggling back and forth.

Great job, Empire. Let's make one of the most terrifying weapons of all time have the maturity of a five-year-old. That's a great idea. I don't want to be there when she finally has a temper tantrum. I hope those faces don't. . . escalate. Well, I knew this was my execution from the beginning . . . But I was really hoping for a different sort of death.

Djaem barely managed to keep his face blank as the doors clanged shut. His stomach felt like it fell through the bottom of his seat as the announcer began to speak. Others were ordering food. *Morons. . . How can you think of food at times like this? How I envy simple minds. Free of anything I can call a thought. . . I'd have so much more time for fun.* His brain tormented him as it went through a list of things that could go wrong. All the possible horrible deaths played on repeat in his mind. The calculations and percentages wreaked havoc with his heart. His whole body clenched as the thrusters kicked on and the shuttle began to move. His eyes were locked on the window that showed the great big nothing. He felt his spine begin to twitch as he watched the ground suddenly rip away, and they were flung from blessed land into the great abyss of space. A tiny speck of dust in a pocket of air surrounded by a vast nothing, waiting to suck him to pieces. Primal terror spun his mind into a frenzy and all reason left him. There was nothing but the inky darkness and the icy cold of the void. *This is hell. I am dead.*

He was in a panicked frenzy, shaking uncontrollably, with tears streaming down from his wide eyes. He was aware of himself but was disconnected. It was as if he were floating above himself, watching from a distance. The other passengers had moved away when his fit had begun with a piercing scream.

Djaem had been in contact with someone almost continually since childhood, like anyone born in the slums of a hive. There had been a time when he longed for privacy. It was not until he received his first brush with being alone that he realized that it was not for him.

It had been some years ago. He had visited one of the

food distributor's offices. The building took up several times its allotted space. While there, he noted how thin the air was. The light air made his heartbeat faster. He had stepped away to calm his heart. After washing off his face, he looked around and saw nobody. There was not a single face anywhere in the room. That is when he panicked. In his frenzy, he overlooked the flat-panel door and couldn't remember how to get out of the room. Screaming and hyperventilating on the floor, he was imprisoned in the restroom for the lesser of eternity or five minutes. The two were as one to him. It was the curse of the hive. The longer you are there, the more you need others around you.

Hive-born were notoriously hard to transport.

Djaem's first trip to outer space had been as a prisoner. It had done nothing to help him overcome his fear.

SCYTHIA WAS EXCITED to go to space, away from the Ethereal soup of the planet. All those people, with their thoughts and emotions congesting the air, made it hard for her to breathe. The Ether had been bursting with them planet-side. There was just too much light, and noise.

Everyone had their own light, their own sound. Most people made a single note, others could play a melody, and very few had a song. Djaem had a symphony: his mind was full of light and gears. All the parts of his shining crystal palace moved and worked like a precision music box. As the ship began to ascend away from the noise of the planet, his music became frantic, shrill, and screeching. Then it simply crashed, all the gears stopped. Now the light flashed a red color like the thrumming heartbeat of a tiny bird. Scythia was stunned into silence as she watched, unsure how to stop his mind from splintering.

Then she heard him scream. He had grabbed the arms of the chair and curled into a terrified ball. At first, she had tried to find the psychic who was hurting her Gem, but then she realized he was doing it to himself. As all the others moved away, she slowly inched closer. She watched the tiny droplets of sweat floating around his face like prisms of dew. She waited until they fell like rain to undo their buckles. The artificial gravity was easier on her than most and she moved with ease.

Raza had to help clear the room as she shook her head with disgust. "Stupid hivers. He should have said it was his first trip. They never handle the shock well." She looked at Scythia. "Get him to the room. He is your handler, which means you have to take care of him too."

Djaem's screams had withered to tiny whimpering. His skin, usually a healthy nut-brown color, was shaded in yellows and greens. She carefully pulled him out of the seat and awkwardly shouldered him out of the shuttle. She shuffled onto the interstellar transport with Raza and Uthraith, tickets at the ready. She didn't notice that all the other travelers waited for them to pass before they dared to step into line.

She carried him and their bags all the way to his room. Her muscles strained under the weight and the bags dragged on the floor behind her. She didn't ask for help. He was her handler; she was supposed to take care of him. The rooms on the transport were not as large as in the dorm. She knew she had her own room down the hall. Djaem had carefully gone over the layout of the halls in detail so she wouldn't get lost. For now, she needed to take care of Djaem.

She closed the shuttle viewing port to the outside and

laid Djaem on his bed. He instantly curled back into the fetal position, his panic continuing.

Scythia's mind was so much clearer as the Ether quieted. They were far away from the roar of the planet now. The huge transport cruiser had thousands of people aboard. Even if it had been packed to capacity, it was barely a ripple in the vast starlit oceans of the Ether. And here in these waters, her mind was a mermaid. Now that she could think, the answers to questions came simpler. She brushed his hair from his sweaty face and peeked inside his mind to find what would make him better. She carefully considered her options on how to solve this problem.

Removing her shoes, she removed his coat and shoes as well, putting him under a blanket. She then emptied their luggage, every scrap of clothing they had went onto a pile on top of him. Scythia then carefully climbed up onto the bed and proceeded to lay down on the top of the clothes pile. She shifted so she was laying along the length of him to provide the maximum amount of pressure she could without causing injury. Once she was in position, she very carefully concentrated on her internal flame and let it burn a little hotter and brighter. It warmed her body as it pressed down on top of Djaem.

I'M ALREADY DEAD. . . I've been executed. I know this. Then why the fuck am I still scared!

Lost inside a cold, endless void, he saw the flicker of light in the distance, a flame dancing at the edge of his vision. He could feel its warmth. He moved with a sluggish, twitching motion toward it. He felt tingling in his fingers and toes. A thousand pins and needles moved up and down his arms. He could feel the warmth around him and a comforting pressure weighing in from all sides. He could feel the breathing of someone else against his back. At that moment it didn't matter who. It was another living being. In the abyss of nothing, it was life. It was another soul. With ungraceful and desperate motions, Djaem forced his limbs to move, rolling over so that he could wrap his arms around this person, clinging to them like a lifeline. Dignity and pride, these things have no value in the void.

SCYTHIA REMAINED LYING there for a long time, letting her mind drift with the Ether around them. She hummed quietly to his mind, trying to help calm the pulsing heartbeat. She smiled as she saw his mind begin to process again. The pulsing red light shifted to a steady deep drumming and then purring as higher brain functions returned.

Scythia watched the wondrous creation of spun-glass spindles, fine crystal cranks, and diamond gears that formed Djaem's mind. It was an amazing machine that could foretell the future. He had a rainbow of lights that scintillated and danced depending on what he was thinking. She liked watching him think. His mind had stopped so suddenly she was afraid it might have broken.

She whispered, "I know what it is like to be lost in dark places. Just follow my light. I will keep my candle burning, so you won't have to be afraid of the dark."

Even as she spoke them, those words echoed back to her. The echo was a memory fragment, like a scrap of chard paper she caught in a breeze. She winced at the sudden stab of pain in her head. With deep breaths she let her mind drift away into the Ether to listen to the songs of the universe. Time means little in the Ether. She had no way of knowing how long it took him to wrap his arms around her torso. Or how long his face was pressed into the crook of her neck. The piles of clothes between them made it so that just his arms and his face were exposed. His hot breath against her skin tickled a little. She smiled as she reached up and petted the top of his head. She mimicked the gesture of comfort they used on her and sighed. If his mind wasn't away, she would give him one of her 'sweeties.' She carefully continued to pet the top of his hair, hoping it offered some of the comfort it made her feel.

IT TOOK a few more minutes before Djaem was able to open his eyes and focus his consciousness enough to realize the precarious position he found himself in. She was humming and her heat was surrounding him. Her long, delicate fingers were gently sliding through his hair. His hands had already pulled her close and were holding her tight. He almost slipped back into his mind to escape reality. *I am clutching the monster that most likely will be my death.*

He tried to pull away, but all that did was make her focus her eyes on him. She made no move to change their position, though she did stop petting his head. He ignored the traitorous part of himself that wanted her to continue. He still couldn't get his hands to let go of her.

She is so much softer than I thought. There is more of her than I expected.

The scent of her and her soap filled his nostrils. His stressed and hyper vigilant mind began to run full tilt through scenarios. There were many ways to turn this moment to his advantage. Even his intellectual mind turned towards more base desires for comfort in a crisis. For a moment he contemplated the many benefits of seduction. It would keep the void at bay, and it was a great way to keep control of a person. Physically, she was lovely. He had never seen anyone like her. He had almost convinced himself that this was the way to go.

"I can see you thinking," she whispered softly to him. "Those are dark thoughts. You don't really want to do that. No fear, Djaem, I won't touch you like that unless you want me to. I promised to keep you from being hurt. That's all I am doing."

Her voice was soft and helped slow his mind. Still, his hands refused to let go.

"Why does this make you feel better? Most would think being covered and pressed would be confining."

His voice was rough, and his throat hurt as he spoke. "On my planet, the people are so tightly packed together you are never really alone. In the poor sections where I am from, you are almost always touching someone. We would sleep all piled up together in the shelter. We form little circles for protection, the women and children in the center, and the men piled up on top of them. After a while it feels odd when you aren't next to someone."

You don't need to tell her your weakness. It's bad enough you are still clutched on like a baby.

She was quiet for a moment as she considered this.

"This is the longest I have ever touched anyone since my beginning." He realized she meant since the training; they really had taken all her memories. She continued to whisper in his ear. "I find it relaxing. When we are in space, I will hold on to you, so you are not alone."

He frowned as he considered the options and this new development. She had no shame, no expectations; she would not ridicule or blackmail him. He couldn't afford to go into a panic-induced coma every time they traveled.

"Yes. I think that would be for the best. So, stay here with me for a while," he said, closing his eyes again. "For the sake of our mission effectiveness, of course." Burrowing against her warmth, he didn't care that it would affect their power dynamic. He would fix it later, but right now he didn't care. He just needed to keep the empty away.

4

TRAVEL, DAY THREE

SWISH, swish, swish.

Click, click. Click, click.

Djaem listened as Scythia approached the bedside. He continued to lay buried beneath a heavy blanket, pretending to sleep.

He had bought those shoes for her right before they left the planet. The heels and toes had little metal tips that made a loud click every time they hit the metal floors. Between the rustling sound of her skirt and the clicking of her shoes, she wasn't able to sneak up on him anymore. She had followed him around almost everywhere before they departed, and he had grown accustomed to the sound.

She lowered herself onto the floor next to his bed and stared intently at his face. Her quarters were down the hall, but since his collapse, she had remained here with him. She made no complaints about any of it. To his relief, she had no sense of personal space, and his irrational need for contact and closeness did not bother her in the slightest.

Secretly he was grateful. He didn't want to think about if she had refused.

This was the third day. He had not yet been able to bring himself to leave the room. He had tried to get himself up and moving. He had tried reasoning with himself, being angry with himself, even trying to frighten himself, but so far nothing got him out that door.

It was the greatest humiliation of his life. He hated it. The feeling of weakness, of needing her. The only thing worse was when she would leave. He could feel the emptiness pressing in. His heart would pound, and he would shake. His mind would spin uncontrollably, and he would suffocate in a room full of air. As awful as that felt, the relief was in equal measure afterwards. . . when she came back. She would let him hold onto her for as long as he wanted, no matter what she had been doing.

They worked together to make him function again. He was able to think now, even when she left the room. As long as he was under the blankets. If she was in the room, he could sit up and read and do his paperwork. Little by little, they worked to get him functioning. It was like learning to walk again. Today, he was quite cross because she had been out of the room, and he had to hide under the covers again. He felt the stinging hot shame sweep over him.

After a moment she sighed. "I know you are awake. I can see you thinking."

With waning patience, Djaem asked from his spot, unmoving, "What do you want, Scythia. I told you, check the data files. I got them for you to answer these questions."

He never should have answered a single question. Her curiosity was insatiable, never ending. The questions had been relentless and expansive. He had finally broken down

and bought her encyclopedia crystals with as much information as he could find on the Empire from the in-ship's
computer. She was studying for hours at a time now.

*It's not too awful, I suppose. . . as long as she doesn't leave the
room.* She tilted her head and smiled as she watched him.
"It's not a question."

He groaned. He gave up and rolled over. He unburied
his face so he could look at her with tired eyes. She was
smiling and pressing her lips together, all excited, like she
had a secret. Her blue cheeks were flushed purple in
almost little heart-shaped patterns.

*Uggghhh . . . How the hell does something so incredibly
dangerous look so damn cute? Especially at times like this.*

"What is it, Scythia?" he said finally, his voice still
rough and grouchy.

She moved her face, shifting so that their eyes lay
perfectly aligned with one another. Her strange black
pupils gazed into him. In the ship's ambient light, he could
almost see the nebulas swirling in their depths. Her breath
smelled sweet. She had been eating candy again.

She had a very serious look on her face. Djaem jumped
slightly as she moved closer and lay down next to him. She
had never moved towards him before. She always waited
for him to move towards her. It was one of the few things
that made this bearable. She was passive. Her stillness
allowed him the illusion of control, even dominancy.

"What are you doing, Scythia?" He barely managed to
keep his voice calm.

"Trust me," she whispered.

She put her finger on his mouth and closed her eyes.
His mind began to try to build scenarios of possibilities.
Any other female he would have thought she was trying to
seduce him, maybe murder him. The way she was
touching him seemed like a manipulative tool. His mind

tried to explain her behavior for three whole heartbeats before it simply gave up and waited to see what happened.

He felt a strange tingle over his skin, not unpleasant; it was soothing, really. The sensation reminded him of home, sleeping on his mat with his bunkmates, all piled together like happy puppies.

He hadn't noticed how warm she was. Did she have a fever? Was she always this warm? He hated space travel. The cold, vacant space. . . so huge and empty. He felt the panic begin to creep up, but he could feel her finger hot on his lips. He reflexively focused on that heat. His muscles relaxed and the tension eased out of his thoughts. His eyes drifted closed for what felt like a moment.

Hours later, he was startled awake when he felt like he was about to kiss a flame. His eyes opened wide, and what he saw would have made him scream if he could have taken a breath.

A monster was right above them. Scythia was awake and watching it. Her body laying down next to him but facing toward the creature. Her face had a hard, dangerous look on it. She was glowing with blue fire, and her hair lifted and swirled with orange flames. It was as if she were floating in a pool of water in the middle of the air. The entire room seemed to be distorted in the same strange dark-tinted water. There was a thrumming noise. The creature passed over them, sniffing back and forth as it went. Its arms and legs, all elongated and distorted. Its body made no sense to his eyes; it kept shifting and changing. Fear held firm to him as he watched the creature move away. Someone screamed in the mists, then another, and another.

His voice was about to join that choir.

Her voice filled his mind. "Don't scream. It will see you. Right now, it only sees me. If you make noise, it will notice you too. It fears me; it is not afraid of you. We are in hyperspace, we hit an Ether pocket. These creatures are looking for psychics. They use them to break out of the Ether to get onto the ship. There are suppressors on so they shouldn't be able to get on board."

It fears you? This is a Tyrling . . . They fear nothing. If one of these got loose on a hive, it means thousands of dead and injured. Even for the military, one can wipe out an entire fire team that was established for their specific destruction.

He felt the panic coming back, and his hand moved slowly, looking for his knife under the pillow. The creature was coming back this way, looking at Scythia.

She frowned as she considered his thoughts, her fire changing colors slightly. "It will learn to fear me very soon."

His mind stopped and cycled on one thought. *She heard that?*

She shifted gracefully. She seemed to be dancing in the Ether water. At the end of her motion, she was straddling Djaem backward, sitting on him. Scythia faced away from Djaem and toward the beast.

The Tyrling stalked towards Scythia, snarling. It opened its maw that was more like a black hole filled with death. It grabbed her shoulders, moving as if to bite her face. Inside the Ether, reality distorted for a moment, which lasted for a blink of eternity. Its frigid darkness collided with her scorching flame. Mist and sparks flew above and around them in a kaleidoscope of colors. Djaem had lifted his hands involuntarily, trying to raise his blade in defense, but was frozen in time as he watched the horrifying beauty of the universe.

The creature's howl caused a ripple in the reality of the Ether, making Djaem bounce on the bed as Scythia floated above. Scythia roared in anger, lifting her hand to touch the creature. Her voice echoed, "I do not fear you; I am not your prey. People fear you. You, who has never known fear. Call me predator, call me teacher. Learn what fear is." She twisted slightly at the waist and put one hand on Djaem's chest and the other remained on the monster.

Power streamed from Scythia to Djaem back to the monster above them. She used Djaem's fear, syphoning it out of him and forcing it into the monster's mind.

Vibrations hit them through the Ether, and her whole body went rigid as she glowed even brighter, her blue, orange fire filling up the darkness. He had to close his eyes against the blinding light. The creatures fled back into the void.

She gasped suddenly for air and fell backwards onto his chest. Djaem caught her in his arm, sitting up slightly to support her limp body. She panted heavily, and a light perspiration covered every inch of her. Her blue skin was flushed purple from exertion. Blood trickled out of her nose and from the corner of her mouth. Even her wild hair was damp with sweat.

He held her there for a long time, his heart beating wildly, his eyes wide in the darkness, with one arm holding her protectively and the other holding the knife at the ready. When the fear had finally passed, he became aware of their position.

He slowly lowered her onto the bed next to him, carefully shifting her legs off him.

Seriously, we are going to have to work on her sexual awareness. Or at least body positioning. At some point, this is going to become a problem.

He tucked her under the covers and went to fetch some water. It wasn't that he was unaware of her, or her. . . attributes. Self-preservation was simply much higher on his list, and his libido had shrunk notably with his 'execution.'

Platonic seemed to be working. For now, the bond was built and that was what mattered. His weakness was forcing her to care for him. This made her wish to protect him. She felt safe around him, she trusted him.

You are just doing your job. Don't over think it. It's important to control such a weapon. Her desire to protect you and listen to you is the whole point. Turn your weakness into a strength. It couldn't have been planned better.

He moved away from her to eat at the table. He was able to sit there for ten minutes before his hand began to tremble. At fifteen minutes, he simply rose and brought his plate to the side of the bed. Sitting so that the side of his leg pressed against her back, he was able to finish eating and even read up on their mission plan.

They had four more days of travel left to go before they reached the colony planet.

Almost there.

FOR THE NEXT THREE DAYS, Djaem and Scythia trained. They practiced moving through the ship. He was able to make a complete tour as long as he held her arm. Whenever it became too much, they would stop, and she would sandwich him between the ship and her body. Djaem made sure it simply looked like they were embracing in a corner. No one outside the team could know of his weakness. He didn't even want Uthraith or Raza to see.

Scythia slowly figured out how to connect their minds so that she could provide the sensation of pressure around him, though it was still hard to do that. More than once, the pressure turned to agonizing pain. For her, it was like trying to fine-tune a dial, with her toes in the dark, while drunk. For Djaem, it was like sitting on the other end of the wire, blindfolded, knowing it could be relief or electroshock.

Only once did she try to gently place physical pressure on him using her mind. With a little warmth added, it could feel like other bodies. Two hours later, Djaem was released from Medical, and Scythia realized how much more complex the physical manipulations were. Both learned. Both grew.

The pain made a great motivator. Soon, Djaem could manage quite a bit, even alone for short periods of time. This link also made it easier for Scythia to tell when the fear was becoming too great. She started to taper the contact she gave, slightly less with each coming panic. Djaem began to dread the comforting link and would push himself harder. Fear could overcome fear.

5

—————————————

DAY SIX, SHIP TRANSFER

THE SLIP-DRIVE of the transport ship powered down and emerged from the Ether. It met with a matter-drive transport as scheduled. They circled and danced around each other before they connected to transfer passengers and supplies. Djaem closed his eyes and walked with his arm tight around Scythia's waist as they went through the flexible tube from one ship to the other.

Djaem may not have been able to navigate the umbilical alone, but he was able to transition by himself once on board.

At least it's a matter-ship. Leaving the hive is bad enough. . . crossing through the slip is just so much worse. He kept his face blank as he considered the new surroundings. The corridors were narrower and there were no view ports to the vastness outside. *Without using the Ether. . . this trip would have taken eight years at sub-light. I'm just glad it's almost over.*

The matter-ship was loaded with asteroid miners recently released on liberty. The loading area was crowded. The press of humanity in tight quarters had Djaem feeling like himself again. He smiled softly as he rolled tension out of his shoulders and went back to work.

SCYTHIA WATCHED in amazement as Djaem approached lifelong friends he was meeting for the first time. Within minutes, the miners were sharing with him things they did not even tell their families. Her eyes followed him as he moved around the crowd. She smiled as she sat on a piece of cargo, her long legs swinging from the edge of the box. She watched a show that no one else could see.

To her eyes, this was a dazzling magic trick with puppets on strings that Djaem moved around. He had observed the miners for just a few minutes before his lights and crystals blazed to life. His music changed tempo to harmonize with the notes around him. He changed the cacophony surrounding them into a lovely rhythm. The colors shifted to compliment his own. Images flickered through his crystal palace until a mirage was conjured and draped around Djaem.

It took Scythia a moment to realize he had disguised himself as one of the masses, blending into their numbers. He spoke as they did, about the same topics. He even used the same slang. She couldn't hear them, but she could see the conversation with blips of color and sound. As the crowd absorbed Djaem, he became the hand inside the puppet. Every change in the discussion was caused by one of his manipulations. His own thought-light would infect and change the thought-lights of others, pulling the strings of his marionettes.

She wondered if she, too, could do this. Without a moment's hesitation, she reached out into the Ether and replaced a thought-light of one of the ship's crew. She swapped it with her desire for more candies. It almost worked. The poor crewman's face fell blank, and he abandoned his post. A few minutes went by, and he had not returned. She realized it did not have the desired effect. It almost worked, but nothing like her Gem. With little more than the shrug of a curious child, she decided she would have to work on that. She gave it no further concern. When the crewman was finally found hours later, he had gorged himself so heavily on raw sugar, he needed two days in the infirmary to recover.

The puppet of humanity, however, obeyed its master in a way she could not hope to achieve. Djaem's thoughts became integrated into the thoughts and feelings of the people he spoke with. His manipulation caused rippling dominos in the minds around him. It did not disrupt their usual self, and this made them fully capable of functioning despite the disruption. They revealed shipping plans and times, names of company administrators, and other bits of useless information Djaem seemed to think were important. What's more, the people revealing this felt happy about doing so.

Looking for a way to help, Scythia found her chance when Djaem was asking about how to get to the colony core. It was behind a locked passage with an access code, and his efforts to get the code were met with nervousness and avoidance. Scythia, with as much effort as goes into wiping your mouth after taking a drink, replaced these feelings with the nervous pride she saw on one of the men who had just become a father. He was eager to see his child for the first time, and maybe this could help Djaem.

"Not everyone knows that code," he said proudly, "and only the most trusted people get access. I served for eight long years before I got this. Leave it in my locker when you're done," he said, handing a surprised Djaem a pass card. "My leave is off-world, anyway."

Don't do that, Djaem hissed at her in his mind. *It will draw more attention to us. I have this well in hand.*

She blinked in surprise. *He has never said that before.* No one had ever scolded her before, not that she could remember, anyway. For a moment she froze as she didn't know how to react. Tears formed at the edges of her eyes as her breathing hastened. She hung her head slightly, looking down at her swishy skirt and clicky shoes. She sniffled slightly as she tried to distract herself with the sound of them. She didn't know why that hurt. She was confused. She pressed her lips together, but it just made her hiccup slightly. *Was he mad? . . . Would he stay mad forever?*

She was frozen, lost in her own world of questions. She didn't understand, much less know how to answer.

"Oh, no. I'll go through channels planet-side. I wouldn't want anyone in any trouble." Djaem returned the card with a smile. The miner took it back with a moment of alarm. As he started thinking over why he would be so careless, Djaem started asking about the local education opportunities. The discussion moved that way, and the nervousness, shock, and alarm all melted to warmth and hope. He really knew how to manipulate them. He saw what they wanted and needed to hear.

As Scythia thought about what she might have done wrong and worried that her Gem might be upset forever, she realized Djaem was suddenly holding a bag of gummy fruit candies in front of her. She looked at him and realized his mind was already past her mistake. With a happy sound, she grabbed them up and smiled brightly. The relief was as surprising as it was complete. Everything was alright. Of course, she had to feed the first one to her Gem.

"But now how will we get in?" Scythia asked curiously.

Raza didn't speak. She simply held out the access card. She had lifted it from Djaem and copied it all in the few moments it took for him to state he was returning it. "Sloppy, Hive-boy. You botched that one good."

Scythia blinked and was surprised to see Raza there. Tilting her head to one side, she realized that her thoughts were muted. . . Hidden as if under a mirror. *What a clever little spider she is. But not clever enough.* A flash of pain for the spider lady. Not enough to bring her to her knees, just enough to remind her, like an echo of the past.

"That is not his name, Raza," she said with an angry face. Scythia leaned forward and put a candy in Raza's mouth when she was about to say something. "But people make mistakes. I forgive you!" she said happily, having learned something new today.

Raza glared at Scythia for a moment and then blew out a breath. "Scythia, it's pointless to be angry at you." She shook her head. "Reign her in," she said to Djaem, though she didn't call him a name this time.

I DIDN'T EVEN HAVE to say it. It's nice having the monster on the leash. Why didn't I sign up for this sooner? Djaem smiled in satisfaction at what he considered his own work. *She's reigned in just fine.*

"Come on, Scythia. Djaem's going to need his teddy bear," Raza mocked as the planet-fall alert-lights came on. *More like grizzly,* Djaem mused.

Scythia was immediately concerned and started looking around for this bear. She began to dig through their bag. "Where is it? It's LOST!"

She grabbed Djaem's arm and said quickly, "Don't

worry, I will find it!" She turned away frantically, searching the ground in long strides. After about twenty paces, she came running back, grabbing his arm again. "What's a teddy bear look like?"

Uthraith laughed openly. His head fell back as his voice boomed out from his belly. "Like you, Little Blue." His lack of concern about manners or offending her showed. The other two managed to hide their amusement.

Scythia was confused for a moment and then nodded slowly. "Oh. . . Okay." Off she went again, disappearing quickly through the crowd and was gone for almost ten minutes.

She came back at full speed, holding out a plush doll of a blue-skinned Star-born with white hair and a long purple gown. She was running full speed with a pair of security guards trying to catch up behind her.

"FOUND IT!" she shouted with triumph.

The other three sat, shocked, in the waiting area. "She actually found it?" Raza whispered.

One guard caught up to Scythia and had a hand on her elbow for almost a full three seconds before he collapsed into a heap. The second guard walked up and glared at the whole group. Lifting his helmet, the grizzled old man missing an eye smirked.

"Good. Now maybe this Gem of yours would be so kind as to pay for the 'teddy bear?' "

The three members of her team stared in confusion. Raza finally closed her mouth and passed over a handful of local credits. "They can keep the change," she said in an almost hollow tone.

Djaem glared at Raza slightly, being the only one to have seen her slip those credits from the guard's belt pouch. He then turned to address Scythia. "Dear. . . he meant. . . I meant you. But. . . I guess this will work."

She tilted her head and looked at Djaem. "Who meant what?" Apparently, she didn't recall how this adventure started or at least was too excited by its completion to think about it.

The guard took the credits, looked at everyone for a moment, and then leaned over to whisper something into Scythia's ear. He was about as tall as she was, but he was much too broad to be a Star-born. She giggled and nodded as he patted her on the head. "Enjoy your trip, miss," he said as he strolled away. His fellow guard limped along behind him.

She sat down next to Djaem and fixed the doll's dress a little, humming as she handed it over. "We will have to fix her hair. It's all wrong."

Djaem smiled amused as he took the doll, he studied the features and agree.

"Of course, dear." He said as he tucked the doll inside his coat for safe keeping.

6

ARRIVAL TO HIVE-MINE: MISSION BEGINS

SHE FELT the hive world long before she saw it. The swarm of humanity droned against the quiet of space, sending vibrations through the Ether. She had never seen anything so loud, or bright. Even the heavily populated planet of the Citadel paled in comparison. The vibrations reached her even beyond its orbit and became more and more disruptive the closer they came. She was able to keep calm as she helped Djaem get closer and closer. This was the place that made her Gem feel safe. She wanted to get him there, but as they reached the planet, the noise of humanity in the Ether was a cacophony against her senses. All their minds talking, crying, happy, sad, love, sex, death. . . It was a pulsating globe of diamond shards scintillating in colors and light.

She looked over at Djaem, whose mind was already swirling and sparkling in anticipation. Even among all these lights, his was still different.

Scythia had studied up on hive worlds to better understand her Gem. This world had been designed as a hive to help with the mining and export of minerals. A swarm was a term used in the Empire to describe the people working in a hive city. They clustered together, buzzing around with both speech and activity. The noisy swirling mess is often too disorienting for those not from hive-type worlds to deal with. The clusters were people working on the project, formed into a small, tightly spaced group. These groups moved amongst each other and collected close to other clusters working on related jobs. Members from one would contact groups on the same or similar jobs, which were spaced in other clusters. Some individuals would pass in between the clusters as part of their role in the swarm. The movements and flow had their own special timing. To those who knew how to read it and who could understand, it is a beautiful thing and easily navigated.

Raza and Uthraith stood in shocked horror, looking across the oozing mass of human beings. The noise was almost music here, people working in harmony and each knowing their place. A buzzing, whirring, dizzying song of life. For Scythia, it was bewilderment.

The people were a tightly packed wall. They flitted about each other with no concern for anyone they might bump into. After a moment, a face popped out, emerging from the nearest body wall. It was Djaem. Scythia hadn't noticed him disappear. The lights and noise had drowned out his music. Raza and Uthraith also seemed surprised to see him.

"Okay, sorry about that. I'll get a lift and make us a path. I'll be right back." Djaem smiled calmly and motioned for them to stay on the platform.

With that, the amoeba of people swallowed him up again. The trio tried to keep him in view. They watched as he moved through this shifting herd effortlessly. As he traveled with confidence, he often squeezed through gaps smaller than himself. Nobody seemed to mind. The people rubbed against one another without notice. Before long, he had disappeared in too deep to be followed. Scythia only knew by his unusual color and her mental link where he had gone. He was a tiny, sparkling fish in an ocean school, and she had the thinnest fishing line attached to him.

"They don't have any," he surfaced with no other announcement. The three jumped, startled, as Djaem appeared to their left. Even Scythia was surprised by his sudden appearance. "We will have to walk it. I can make a little bit of a path, but you'll just have to tough it out."

Raza gave a disgusted grunt, and Uthraith made an audible growl. Both moved items from their pockets to their hands to keep them from pickpockets. Scythia, however, continued to stare across the crowd. Her expression fell somewhere between vacancy, amazement, and revulsion. All too quickly, they began their trek through the gauntlet.

She watched as Djaem again worked his magic. Often without words, his approach would get small openings to form in the crowd. When these openings were too small, Uthraith growled or shouted, and that widened them a bit more. Even with this, the swarm pushed to resume its original form. The paths collapsed back on themselves quickly, and the Hive-men did not appreciate the disruption. Djaem never slowed. He was trying to get them through this area as fast as possible. He was moving quickly, too quickly.

Those that crushed up against Raza were tased. When Uthraith was pushed too far, he would grab and throw the offenders. This created a violent and resentful wave that rippled through the crowd.

The one most affected by it, however, was Scythia. When the swarm closed on her, she not only heard and felt them, but their thoughts and voices were filling her up, drowning her own voice. She was being scolded dozens of times by many angry voices. . . Those voices were followed by the silence of her own. The swarm was a swirling mass of chaos that her mind began to emulate. It was confusion, annoyance, and pain. When Uthraith acted violently. . . It was anger. But there was something else here. There was something underneath, seething. A subtle voice in the chaos. Watching. . . waiting. . . malicious.

"Too much," she gasped, but her words were muted by the buzzing crowd. She tried again, a little louder. Djaem could not hear her over the noise.

Uthraith, however, glanced down when she called out a third time.

"HANDS OFF HER!" he roared his voice booming over the crowd. He shifted his large frame and encircled her with his arms. He flung an offending swarmer. Scythia felt the surprise. . . the fear. . . the anger.

Then, the buzzing stopped. Scythia screamed as she grabbed her head. Her grasp of herself slipped and instinct took over for the space of a heartbeat. She lashed out. An entire cluster, including her own team, stumbled as a sudden burning pain exploded out from her. She was not yet able to open her eyes when a hand grabbed her. She moved the focus of the pain to that grasping hand, but its grip did not relent.

"Focus on me," Djaem's voice gritted through the pain. "Focus on me. . . Share my mind. We have to move, or they will swallow us up." His legs buckled under the force of her focus. His ability to reason saved him. He knew where his body ended and was able to ignore the over-whelming pain that came from beyond that point.

She grabbed hold of that lifeline, the little connection she had with him. Her mind was lost in the swamp of their collective consciousness. It was gasping for air but choking on thick mud.

"I AM DROWNING. . ." She had no idea she was screaming. The noise was so loud in her head. She curled into a ball as she clutched onto Djaem's arms. Her eyes opened wide with only the pale whites showing as she convulsed. Her whole body heaved as it tried to spit out the Ether. In a desperate attempt to save herself, she bit down on her own arm. Blood filled her mouth. The physical pain allowed her to focus. Suddenly, she was her own flesh and blood again. She focused on Djaem's mind. Red tears trailed down her blue cheeks. She thrust her body forward, curling around Djaem. She shuddered as she released the pain. Instead, she tried to find a way to shield herself. She had never before tried to close herself off from the Ether. She tried to create a bubble of safety. She whimpered Djaem's name as she tried to hide. She curled into a ball, desperate to keep her face out of the ocean around her. She buried it into Djaem's chest, holding tightly to him.

OUT OF REFLEX more than design, Djaem wrapped his arms around her back. He was surprised she could become this small. Her body length should have made it impossible, but she practically folded in on herself.

Her little explosion had caused quite a stir in the crowd. Although the cluster had given them a little breathing room, it didn't give them much time before they pressed back in, angry and violent.

Djaem gathered her up into his arms. He dashed frantically through the crowd. He moved like a gazelle running from lions, swift and nimble. He was almost at a full sprint through the swarm. He was able to move as if they were not there. The swarm responded to him, making openings moments before he arrived, and it closed as soon as he passed. Raza and Uthraith tried to keep up and came to understand why it had been so difficult to apprehend him.

A black suit finally came into view at the far end of the docking bay. The man was tall and slender and openly armed. His gaze had been scanning the crowd but finally rested upon the two approaching. He gripped his weapon tightly.

"There are supposed to be four?" The man was unknown to Djaem, but he had been told where to find the special handlers for this mission. This was where they were to meet them.

"The other two will catch up. I have to get her out of here. Where's your office? Turn the suppressors on."

They stepped quickly into an office. Scythia was still locked in her panicked mind. Djaem was sore and out of breath. His arms burned from carrying her weight. She wasn't as heavy as he had expected. Star-born are less dense than Planet-born. Even so, it was far more than he had ever attempted to sprint with.

The man did not speak again; he simply opened the door and placed his thumb on a scanner next to the door. Djaem waited for her body to relax and her breathing to even. He continued to hold her up until her feet sank down towards the floor of their own accord.

RELIEF! Scythia was finally able to think again. The oppressive noise began to rapidly recede as the suppressors did their job. Even though the suppressors were not strong enough to stop Scythia's power altogether, they allowed her to gain control. She gasped out in relief, blinking her eyes as she looked at her new surroundings.

A sound of clicks startled her, and she realized it was her own feet touching the metal floor. Her mind began to catch up and process what had happened. An exhausted, sweaty Djaem finished gently placing her into a chair before practically collapsing in front of it. He took deep, sucking breaths of air as he rested against her knee.

He carried me. That's why he's exhausted.

Her hands trembled as she reached out and touched Djaem's cheeks. Her whole body felt thin and fragile. The swarm of humanity was a turbulent ocean crashing against the walls of this office. She could hear it pounding, but here she could breathe. She folded herself forward, leaning so that they were eye to eye. She focused on her breathing and then on him. It was a simple meditation. She couldn't remember how or where she learned it. She still had fragments of those memories from before, where she used it when she was alone. As she counted and measured each breath, Djaem began to do the same in response. His breathing became less labored, and the flush left his face.

Suddenly, Scythia noticed Djaem's irises were a mix of different shades of brown swirled together. His lashes were curled and just slightly darker than his pupils. He had the faintest crinkle at the corner of his eyes. For the first time she saw him without the Ether overlapping. She softly cupped his cheek. She was surprised at the rough texture of his skin. She looked at the contrast of her blue and his brown skin. She gave him a soft, exhausted smile and closed her eyes in the meditation. This allowed her to control her power for the delicate task of pulling at the Ether in the room. She pulled the string of energy through herself and into him, then back again.

Energy. . . the great, indestructible, interchangeable,

unstoppable force flowed from one being to the other in a circle, refreshing them both.

Neither Djaem nor Scythia noticed when the man in the black-armored suit nodded. Djaem was only vaguely aware of when the man stepped back out through the door, leaving them alone.

7

MISSION DAY ONE

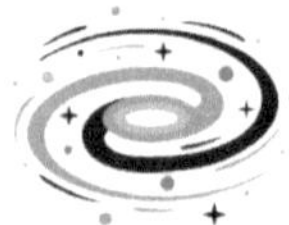

AN ANGRY VOICE pierced the walls of the small office. "But did you have to shoot him?"

The door slid open, revealing the man in the black armored suit. His visor was up, allowing him to glare angrily at a grinning Uthraith and an annoyed-looking Raza. "Come on! You're overreacting. Just admit it!" Raza snapped back at him.

"Explosives are expressly forbidden on the colony beyond the deep mines." His voice fell into a self-mutter. "Why did they send me these ones. . .?"

This should be easy, Djaem thought. "So, you are Artos? The one we are supposed to talk to about the Ether wave, right?"

The man removed his helmet and dragged a hand through his hair. He looked as if he might cry from frustration. He pressed a button on the wall and secured the door. He silently made his way to his desk and sank into his chair. His hand covered his face as he took a deep breath, trying to calm himself. "Do any of you know what the word 'classified' means?"

Scythia raised a hand with just the slightest tremor. In a shaking, little-girl voice, she said, "To classify is to put a person, place, or thing into a categorical or topical format based on distinguishing traits." She recited the answer that she had found in the data crystals.

She gave the man a smile even though she was still shaking from shock. What Artos returned to her was a growling scowl. Raza hid her grin in her hand. Uthraith laughed out loud, beaming proudly.

"Your office isn't secure? Then, we're done here," Djaem snapped dismissively. He managed to sound arrogant even as he picked himself up from his undignified position on the floor. He headed straight for the door. There was a heavy thud when he continued walking without it opening automatically.

Scythia did not get up from her chair.

"I hadn't yet locked it down," taunted Artos from his desk. "Now if we are ready. . ." Several screens lit up, and he began shuffling through paper folders with pictures of each of the four of them on the covers. While reading from each, he glanced up at the pictured person and grumbled.

"I have done some of your work for you. You will need to identify the source—" he started before Raza cut him off.

"Source of the energy, which is slightly into the deep mines." She grinned at him. Artos did not look pleased.

"Yes. . . and to get there you will need—" Raza held up the active security card. "And you should—"

"Meet with Guardsman Evers. Do you have any actual information, or are we wasting our time?" Djaem sounded less than amused as he rubbed his forehead, where a bump was forming.

"Uhh. . ." Artos grabbed back up the two files and

started flipping through them again. "Well. . . this entire mission is classified. And. . . try not to. . . do too much damage." He gritted out in pained frustration.

Uthraith and Scythia simply smiled. Djaem was deeply unsettled by how alike those smiles were.

THE TINY DOMICILE cubes were packed so tightly together, they formed the walls of the city. In comparison with the inside of the homes, the outside was expansive. Djaem thought of the streets as empty, but it was a relative term. Parents, children, miscreants, and security all roamed the wide roads. The education centers and distribution offices buzzed with activity, but the hundreds currently active were nothing compared to the tens of thousands these roads were built to accommodate.

CLI-CLICK SWISH. Cli-click swish. Scythia had seen a new game from the children in front of the introductory educational facilities. They called it step-skipping, or just skipping. It made the most of the clicky-ness of her shoes and the swishy-ness of her dress. She smiled as she skipped along with the team, but there was little joy in it. Drowning in the sea of honey that was the mind of this swarm still clung heavily to her. It was like a nightmare that haunted her during the daylight hours.

Her mind turned and twisted around as she pondered what had happened. What makes a person? If it is their personality, where does that come from? Does it come from their experiences? Aren't experiences just the memories of what has happened to that person? If that were true, then it is memories that make up a person. Her memories made up less than a month. This lack-of-self allowed her to float through the Ether with ease. Like a ghost, she could pass among people, looking in and feeling those memories and emotions. However, it meant she had no armor, no shield to keep them out when they all pressed in around her. She was terrified that she would simply cease to be. She couldn't let on to this, though. The others seemed to be in lighter spirits whenever she was fun-loving. She had learned quickly they preferred their weapon happy rather than frightening. She wanted to please them and so kept her face in a happy smile, bouncing along. The new skip helped keep her in the Here and now.

UTHRAITH PLODDED ALONG, carrying all the equipment the entire group had requisitioned. He didn't mind. In fact, he barely noticed. The entire pack weighed barely more than a man. Watching the people puzzled him, as did the layout of the buildings. They grew into each other and fused into one. The sun could barely reach the ground here. Everything looked dirty and burnt. And the smells. . . He could identify the smell of human overpopulation, but this went far beyond that. Tar, smoke, chemicals. It was horrible and putrid. He smiled as he considered the many ways, he could help this colony. If only one person in a thousand survived, they could live actual lives. Maybe they could even grow a plant. LSAPO tanks were where places like this one and most spacecraft got their oxygen; he was familiar with the stink. Out in the Reaches, you get oxygen from the plants. This place needed plants. . . and humans make excellent fertilizer.

RAZA WAS HAVING her own difficulties. She was born out in the feral Reaches of space, same as Uthraith, and noted many of the same things. However, she did it without his morbid conclusions. She shared life on city streets with Djaem and recognized the threats to the mission and their safety. It was causing her to develop a nervous tick. She repeatedly flicked the switch of the knives she carried, rapidly heating the blades, then cutting power and regenerating the heat back into the battery over and over as they walked. Hot–cool. . . Hot, cool. . .

THE U.L.A (UNIVERSAL, Law, Authority) militia took note of their passing. A psychopathic Star-born, a cannibalistic tribal giant, and street scum from the Reaches, all made their way through the city. The group was being watched heavily; but for a lack of courage, the guards would have approached to challenge their intentions. The more perceptive guards also noted that there was something missing from this ragtag band.

DJAEM HAD ALREADY MADE his departure from the group. No one had noticed him when he was still with the group. No one noticed when he left either. He went ahead to gather information on the mine master while his team naturally created a distraction. After a quick stop by the master's residence, he realized the only leverage would be with his associates. The master's apartment was beyond scant. It measured twelve feet deep by eight feet wide, held a bed with an integrated dresser, a wall-mounted television, a sink and toilet, and a fold-out range. He didn't even have a refrigerating unit. Shaking his head in disgust, Djaem left silently. *If the master is this deep in poverty. . . how do the workers even survive?*

He left quickly, heading immediately for the transfer gates. He knew the path he had set up for his companions would give him a few extra minutes to complete his tasks. This was the first mission of his execution, and things were already going wrong. Even for a dead man his future did not look bright. There were many fates worse than death in the Empire. Djaem had no wish to make his any worse.

"ZAH! HE IS THERE!" Uthraith pointed out the small group of people gathered at the large shipping gates. He often forgot that he was more than a foot taller than all of his companions. His size allowed him to see over obstacles they could not. It was a more crowded part of the city, and a small, flowing herd occupied the streets. Once past that crowd, however, the area a hundred feet out from the gates was wide open. It was like fording across of rive of flesh. A frown came to his face as he looked down at Little Blue. Even as spindly and tall as she was, he still hung above her. He read the stiffness in her shoulders and awkwardness of her movements. She pretended that she wasn't on the edge of panic. Uthraith had survived countless battles by following his razor-sharp instincts. He wasn't about to ignore them now.

"Move!" Uthraith's voice boomed at the people. He lengthened his steps to increase his pace. He didn't want Little Blue to have another fit. The herd parted for him.

DJAEM WAS LEANING against the wall on one arm while talking to the least filthy man they had seen since leaving the spaceport. He was short and looked as though he were once very heavily muscled, but time and light work had softened him. The other two were guardsmen. One guard stood confidently, rifle holstered, and in a position to protect Djaem. He seemed more familiar and comfortable with the off-worlder than the city official he was supposedly ordered to protect.

Everyone had different reactions. Raza was impressed at how quickly Djaem had inserted himself into the world here, as if he had always been a part of day-to-day. Uthraith barely registered anything except impatience to be done with this place. Scythia was just genuinely relieved to reach Djaem again. She didn't stop moving forward until she wrapped her arms around him from behind. She tried hard not to interrupt his conversation. She gave a sigh of relief; she felt like she had been treading water and finally reached a resting place. She set her chin on top of Djaem's head.

Scythia became distracted by an amazing exchange only she could see. The team may have noted that the second guardsman was looking fatigued, wobbling in place, leaning, and eventually sitting down. The helmet he wore hid his face, but had it been visible it would have been much more telling. Only Scythia's Ethereal eyes could see the dance he was in. Her recent trauma was temporarily forgotten, and she could not suppress a giggle.

Djaem was working his magic again. He had taken over the entire flow of the conversation and was steering it exactly where he wanted it to go. The distribution official was apprehensive and aware of the manipulation but kept finding himself relaxing further and further. Every time he noticed, he exuded a burst of anxiety and distrust, which Djaem's mind-lights quickly brushed away. The first guardsman had no way to resist these manipulations. Djaem had him completely enrapt. The real dance was with the shaky guardsman. This was the one that interested her the most.

The second guard was a minor psychic. It was his own Ethereal manipulations that were affecting his mind. A strange, twisted, back-fed mental loop. His psychic training enabled him to resist being swayed by her Gem. Even with his training in place, he frequently had to adjust his own thoughts back to a set he had written in the Ether ahead of time. It was as if he had to restart his mind over and over. More humorous than this was when he would try to adjust Djaem's thoughts. He would reach out through the Ether to add, remove, or change one of her Gem's thought crystals. Scythia remembered what that had done to the transport guard. The spinning, shining mechanisms of Djaem's mind, however, would almost immediately compensate by removing it or replacing it with one exactly as it was before the tampering.

This one is pretty good, Djaem mused to himself, *but I've dealt with psychics before. Since I am always planning, always adjusting, he can change all he wants. I'll spot the weakness in my plan and fix it.*

Scythia could hear Djaem because of their earlier connection. The funniest part to Scythia was when the guard tried to read Djaem's thoughts. He only tried this twice. At first, he had just skimmed the surface. He was looking for Djaem's inner monologue, the thoughts that Scythia could hear like whispers. The guard gasped, collapsing back into his chair, activating his oxygen supply, and sealing himself in his suit. The guard found himself bombarded with a flood of thoughts, each one far beyond his comprehension. Djaem's mind was an open book. Any pressure whatsoever was the same as jumping all the way in at the deep end. The guard had the good sense to steady himself for the next attempt.

His next attempt was to look deeper than Djaem would be conscious of. Some people learned how to cycle thoughts on the surface to prevent psychics from reading them. This poor, unfortunate soul thought he knew the best way around this defense. What he discovered was more than he could handle. First, Djaem honestly looked at himself as a deadman. This was a serious threat, as reading the dead can leave the psychic trapped in the void. Djaem could feel the touch in his mind and the burst of fear from the psychic. The malice that followed would have shown Djaem as a monster to anyone. Scythia watched with interest as the little psychic struggled in the shining crystal maze that formed Djaem's inner workings.

Djaem focused on the disturbance in his mind, severing the escape path for the guardsman. Now, he focused in on the trapped psychic. Unlike most people, Djaem did not need to turn thoughts into words, then move the words to his mouth. He didn't need to wait for this listener to convert them from words to understanding. Everything he said to the guard was transferred at the speed of thought.

"Shit! He's one, too?" Raza watched in surprise as Djaem stopped speaking and the guardsman began to convulse. Gurgles and wet coughing came from within the helmet until he was finally able to pull it off. Blood covered the visor and ran from his eyes, nose, mouth, and ears. At first Raza thought it was Scythia's doing. However, she noticed the same surprise mixed in with Scythia's amused smile. Raza became certain Djaem was unleashing a terrible psychic attack on the guard. She even considered the possibility that Djaem had used poison.

"No," Scythia answered Raza in a soft and calm voice. To Djaem she whispered. "You should let him go." A feeling of compassion for the guard arose from nowhere inside Scythia. Perhaps it was because she so recently experienced drowning in someone else's mind. Mercifully, Scythia turned off the consciousness of the guardsman and then cast his mind next to his body in the Ether. To everyone else's eyes, her hair fluffed in a nonexistent breeze, and the guard fell to the ground, barely breathing.

With the disturbance over and no compassion for the man who intruded on his personal thoughts, Djaem returned to the conversation as if nothing had happened at all. It didn't take long for him to get the information he needed now. One mine had fully breached the mantle of the planet and was shut down. Two more were in danger of a breach. The remaining four mines were still active.

Raza presented the pass card, and Djaem showed his inspector badge. They were allowed to pass with no further incident. A smaller door was opened in the massive metal gates to let them through.

"Leave him there till he gains consciousness, or the monsters will find him before he can find his way back to himself." Scythia warned with a small smile as she passed the remaining guard. He nodded in fear looking down at his unconscious fellow. That guard and those on shift watched as the crew of monsters entered the city's core.

MISSION DAY ONE, THINGS ARE GOING WELL

THE GATES WERE NOT JUST for traffic control; they separated two distinct worlds. All except Djaem thought they had entered an enclosed complex. The inner core was sparse in comparison to the outer ring, allowing for a view of the planet itself. The sun was finally able to kiss the ground over the shorter, less congested buildings. The sky was only visible overhead as the high walls of the surrounding ring created an artificial horizon. The buildings ranged in size and function with walkways between them. The biggest difference, however, was the people.

They were clean, well dressed, and healthy compared with the outer-city dwellers. They did not touch each other often and seemed to understand personal space. The team's business here was short but utterly important. They needed to talk to Guardsman Evers about the Tyrling sightings. This was the safest way to get into the mines. If there was an Ether breach, the source of the Tyrling energy would be in the mines.

While there were some residential buildings, shopping centers, and recreational halls here, distribution warehouses dominated the cityscape. Raza was glad they had arrived in between the daily distribution times. The long lines would have clogged the area and delayed their travel. They had called it the rat-hall when she was a child. There had been a number of reasons for this moniker, the first and foremost being that it was the only building where rodents resided. The empire always kept the ration warehouses with the inner circles, close to the guard houses. Officials said it was to prevent theft and insure there was enough for everyone. Raza knew the truth: it was always about control. *Starving people riot, hungry people stand in line, clever people hunt the rats.* The empire had perfected the art of keeping the population just shy of desperate.

While Raza's mother had stood in line to claim their daily ration, she and her brother had spent that time catching the fat vermin. She suppressed her revulsion at the sight of the centers and focused on following Djaem through the streets.

Djaem sneered as he passed. On his planet the food centers were in heavily guarded bunkers. He had grown up listening to the bloody tales of riots that resulted from food shortages. They had been used to justify the militarization of the inner core. He knew it was just an excuse for corrupt officials to keep the people dependent. Djaem had learned young how to use the corruption of the officials.

SCYTHIA WAS HANDLING this area much better. She was even genuinely enjoying her skipping. Everyone seemed more relaxed, which put her at ease. Until she heard the scream. It was a high-pitched, piercing scream that only the very young managed to produce. It cut through the humming and buzzing of the Ether. The sound resonated with something deep inside her, the echo of some past sound.

She stopped in her tracks. Her whole body stilled as she tilted her head, listening. She turned herself this way and that way, trying to find the direction of the scream. She closed her eyes and focused on the resonating echo.

What is it now, Djaem growled in his head. She did not hear him; her mind had already slipped into the Ether. Searching through the murky depths, it didn't take her long. They screamed again. There were two voices crying in unison, one small, and one large. She moved forward, following the sound of the cries. Her feet clicked faintly in the faraway place of her body. She had to change direction several times. The sound of the cry shifted with the echoes caused by the physical obstacles in her way. Her companions shouted and complained, but their voices were distant and faint. She ignored them.

This cry, it is desperate. . . urgent. The sound tugged at her scarred mind. She knew that sound. *Is it my voice? Is it a voice I know? What? What is it!*

She picked up the pace, her shoes clicking rapidly as she turned left then right. Diving deep into the maze of the back streets, she braced herself against the hum of those around her. Fortunately, the core was free of the crowds they found in the outer hive. Her mind was once again backed by her natural confidence. She charged ahead, secure in her mental fortress. Nothing was going to stop her.

The screams brought her to a place full of voices, crying, praying, and begging. In the Ether, it was a nexus. Dozens of strange Ethereal tethers were secured and heading out in all directions. She reached out to touch one of the strange cords that floated out into the Ether. She realized that these were connections between people, similar to the connection she had developed with Djaem. She could touch the minds of the people attached to either end. This one was the connection between a mother and her child. Her eyes widened as she felt the bond between them. The agonizing loss, the confusion, and fear of the child on the other end. Tears slid out of her eyes unnoticed as she felt their pain. She touched another and another. They were all the same.

She realized at that moment that she didn't have this connection. The echo, maybe it had been her own voice or her mother's. But now nothing remains. *No way to know. Now there is only ashes.* Something deep inside of Scythia ignited. One hand stroked along the brightest of the cords. The most recent to pass this way. She followed it to the warehouse door.

The door was a metal alloy, heavily reinforced. The warehouse walls were thicker and denser than the walls of other buildings in the area. The structure was closed and locked by heavy industrial-grade bolts. It would have taken an industrial saw an hour to cut through it.

Scythia looked down at the object barring her way and ordered, "Stop," her voice low and deep. The sound of a metallic snap could be heard as metal bent to the force of her will. . . just like everything else. A smile that was more than a little sinister spread across her face.

THE OTHER MEMBERS of her team had been following along hastily, trying to keep up and keep people out of her way. Nobody understood what she was doing.

"Reign her in!" Raza had hissed, as if Djaem had some way of making her stop or even explain herself.

"Look at her. She's tracking something," Djaem

replied, analyzing Scythia's face the best he could. The expressions he could normally read so easily were distorted. She was interacting with the Ether, so they made no sense to him. "Maybe she has the scent already. The Tyrling could be near!" Djaem felt fear crawl along his skin at the idea.

"Nuh!" barked Uthraith. "Look at her face. This has been seen before. There will be blood. She is the animal, last of her cubs."

"Can you *try* to make sense," scolded Raza, glaring at her giant.

"She hunts, yes. But this is a hunt to protect. She will not stop. Not until the weak are made safe." With that, he drew his pylon rifle.

"Yes. . . yes, I can see it. It's far more primal than I. . ." Djaem's voice trailed into his own thoughts. His worry grew exponentially. He recalled the tantrum that had been brought up as a joke before. If this was the day he finally saw it, he knew it would be his last.

"Psycho psychic and a helpless handler. . . They ain't paying me enough for this. . .," Raza grumbled, and drew her blades, nonetheless. They all paused briefly to look amongst each other as the lock ripped open. The metal bent and twisted. No one gave voice to the thought they all shared. Was there a lock that could stop their little blue monster? They quickly hurried inside.

INSIDE THE DIMLY LIT WAREHOUSE, Scythia saw two men holding a cargo crate between them. The Ethereal cord led directly to the container. She moved forward with slow, deliberate steps.

Click-clack. Click-clack. Swish. Click-clack. Click-clack. Swish.

The men had stopped at the sound of the lock, turned at the sound of her shoes against the metal floor. Setting down their cargo quickly, one pulled a gun. "Get the fuck outa here out-worlder. Ain't your business." The barrel of his gun gleamed in the light as he growled and took one step towards Scythia.

She had one hand up in the air, touching the Ether cord. "No more crying," she whispered to the minds attached to it. Her eyes found the first of the two men. "Stop," she said in the same tone she used on the lock.

She wasn't sure if she meant stop talking, stop threatening, or stop stealing children. In her mind she just wanted him to stop.

He bent to her will just as everything else did. He stopped everything, all at once. Without a sound his body stopped all its functions, crumpling in a heap. Months later, the scientist of the colony would still be studying his corpse because it would not start natural decomposition. In the present his body crumpled to the floor.

"That's new," she whispered in surprise at his heap. She looked at the second man and became aware of other people in the warehouse. The sound of guns being drawn and charged followed as they turned their attention to Scythia.

Her voice was a deadly whisper in the warehouse air. "Your time is forfeited."

She stepped forward. Click clack swish. The second man tried to fire his gun, but it bent to her will and jammed. His breath came out in a small fog as the air dropped in temperature.

Scythia was completely unaffected by what was

happening around her. She was focused on the task at hand. She ripped open the first container, breaking the industrial-grade locks and awaking the child inside. She gently touched the little girl's head for just a moment before moving away. She followed the next cord to its container and then the next, opening them one after another.

She was either unaware or unconcerned about the armed men. With long determined strides, Scythia made her way across the warehouse as the air erupted into bloody chaos all around her.

UTHRAITH AND RAZA exploded into motion without hesitation. Uthraith's gun boomed, flashing with blinding muzzle flare as his controlled bursts killed the three men farthest back. His movements were calculated to position his body to block any shots that might be fired at Scythia.

Raza became a shadow of death, dancing in the strobe lights that Uthraith's shots created. In the light of each flash, she appeared somewhere new, spinning, twirling, and jumping. Posed like a fragment of motion as someone else was falling. Her deadly art painted the walls and floor with blood.

Djaem, for his part, managed to not get hurt. He threw himself behind the nearest cargo crate, pulling a frightened child out of the fire line.

Shit, shit, shit, shit. . . He picked up a gun and even managed to fire it several times. *Oh, thank the Powers.* To his relief, none of the rounds struck any children or his team. *Well, that's better than the firing range. This thing is wasted on me.* He set the handgun down and pulled out his round underhand knife. The little girl next to him, at the tender age of eight or nine, grabbed the gun and opened fire on a man coming from a side doorway. Djaem flinched back in surprise, looking from the dead man to the girl.

"Well then, let's get the others, shall we?" he said over the noise of the dying. He decided it would be more help to get the children out of the way. Djaem was more familiar with bar brawls, and knife fights. Right now, broken bottles just did not seem appropriate.

SCYTHIA REACHED the rear of the building, moved two rows down, and started coming back up along the line of cargo. The crates were designed to withstand the vacuum of space and were equipped with fusion-enhanced steel locks. They popped open around her like they were on springs.

Her hair glowed with orange fire as it floated and swirled around her head as if underwater. Her feet were no longer actually touching the ground as she stepped. Her breath came out in a fog as ice formed beneath her. Most psychics only ever have one of these signs appear when they use the strongest of their abilities. Using the Ether was dangerous and draining, but she didn't even seem to notice.

A MAN far up in the rafters had seen what became of the first two men. He knew that Scythia was the greatest threat in the room. He positioned and steeled himself to take aim at her blue chest. Calming his breath, he took his shot. His rifle flashed.

This was the day his courage would earn him a great honor. The bullet flashed and buried itself deep into flesh.

Uthraith dodged into the path of the bullet, taking the shot in the center of his chest. He grunted in pain and looked down at the tiny hole. He smiled widely, a laugh burst from his throat, and he chuckled as a tiny trail of blood trickled from the wound. He looked back up at the shooter, lifting a hand towards him. The toughened hide of his skin and subdermal armor was barely phased by the wound. Uthraith spread his feet apart and took a wide stance. Opening his hand from around the rifle in an exaggerated gesture was part of the ritual for his people. It was a ritual that Uthraith had done many times in battle. As he began to draw the small, oval-headed axe, the gunman started shooting again in a frantic spray. Uthraith's joyous laughter could be heard over the noise of the gunfire.

Djaem and Raza were both frozen at the impossible sight. Uthraith had the speed and agility to block every bullet moving towards his head or torso, receiving only one additional bullet in his arm and another in his leg. These wounds did not slow the dash or leap towards the gunmen. They did not weaken the strike that shattered the terrified gunmen's rifle. They did not keep Uthraith from grabbing the man's armor and lifting him into the air.

"You are worthy," Uthraith exclaimed to the man. "My blood is spilt, so there will be honor in your death." Uthraith was overjoyed.

Raza, who had seen this ritual before, moved away. Djaem was staring, his mind trying to process the giant's speed. His brain was still calculating the physics of it all when the 'honoring' ritual began. This particular ritual involved removing the skull of the honored enemy while they are still alive. Djaem cursed himself for his gaping mouth. The man was still screaming as Djaem choked and spat out blood and viscera. He barely kept from retching. *That taste will be with me for a long time.*

THE SKIRMISH WAS over within minutes. Scythia finished freeing up the children. She floated along as she herded them into the wider area of the loading bay. Thirty children of varying ages encircled her. The older children helped by carrying babies in their arms.

In the Ether Scythia gathered the cords and sent a signal, a call to the mothers connected on the other end, summoning them to come and claim their little ones. Scythia focused on leading the mothers to their offspring. Even mothers that had given up hope felt the sudden draw. The thinnest of strands brightened and flared with renewed vigor.

RAZA LOOKED around at the dead, searching their pockets quickly. Little in the way of identification but she was quick to figure out that they were about to ship these crates off-world to distant colonies.

She sneered and spat upon the floor. "Slavers." She had a special kind of hate for slavers. "They often come to the outer colonies and steal women and children. On hives like this it is easy to slip victims away unnoticed. That infant is less than six months old." She wiped her blades clean on her nearest victim.

Uthraith field dressed and wrapped up his prize with a few chunks off the dead man. "Why take them so young? No good as workers. Weak," he asked Raza as he began to reload his weapons.

As Raza walked towards Djaem, watching Scythia, she answered Uthraith. "It's easier to train them, and they won't remember much at this age. Their wills are easier to break and manipulate."

She looked between Scythia and the door. "Look, I don't know what she is doing. But we need to move; the guards will be here any minute."

Uthraith smiled and rolled his neck a little. "Good. Trip was boring."

Raza glared at Uthraith a bit. "This is not part of our mission."

Uthraith shrugged and gave a cheek wiggle of his eyebrows. "So, bonus?"

She rolled her eyes in exasperation. *Sometimes my monster is just as hard to reign.* She looked at Djaem. "He will kill everyone that attacks us. We need to move, unless we want to create a hiring surge in the security department."

SCYTHIA WAS SATISFIED. The mothers were on their way, and the children would soon be reunited. A longing welled up inside her, alien and unfamiliar. Before she had a chance to ponder it, something more familiar caught her attention.

Djaem's thought crystals flashed out beyond the loading bay and then started swarming about the children as he hatched a plan.

"Too late!" he said simply. Tossing a tracking device to Uthraith, he added, "Just meet up with me. No matter what you hear me say, get out of here and get to the rendezvous."

Raza and Scythia looked around to try to spot what he saw, but the incoming guardsmen were not yet in line of sight. Uthraith didn't bother he caught the tracker and tucked it in his pocket. He headed to the back of the warehouse. "This way. I make door."

Raza and Scythia moved away, but Uthraith shouldered his rifle. He winced and recoiled as an unexpected pain shot through his nose and eyes. Momentarily blinded, he growled, "Fa' acy! What's wrong with you?" he turned to glare at Raza.

Raza grimaced, shaking out the hand that stung from hitting the barrel of his gun. "Did you hear him? Djaem has a plan. I've learned to trust this." In that moment, Scythia's mouth grew into a broad grin that seemed to belong on someone else's face. As Raza finished speaking, "Shia mah! Withdraw and rendez. . ." She realized the problem after all: this wasn't Uthraith's first language. "Uh . . . Follow him. Fuck my luck with these idiots."

Scythia's whisper was all but unheard. Accented the way Djaem speaks, she gasped, "Victory." Their minds still connected even at such a distance.

Scythia smiled, pleased with the sounds of the Ether. The hive was humming again. Uthraith was pleased as well with his prize. Raza was just glad to be moving and that no one had been arrested. They were here on official duties, but the backlash with interfering with local security could get messy.

9

MISSION DAY ONE, AND IT'S ALREADY OFF THE RAILS

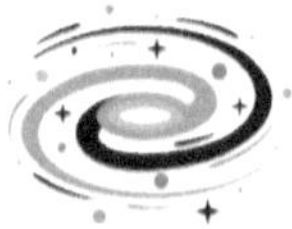

DJAEM HAD SEEN other people moving at windows, closing blinds, or moving away from the streets. Using the reaction of others, he could see far beyond that which lay before him. He ran quickly to place himself between the nearest security group and the children. He already had a well-devised plan. When the security patrol first rounded the corner, Djaem called out, "Minions, slow them down!" This turned him into the primary target.

As soon as the guards arrived, Djaem ran through the group of children. While Djaem sprinted through the crowd, the guards slowed to avoid knocking anyone over. By the time they made it to the rear of the warehouse where Djaem had exited, he was almost three blocks away. He could have easily slipped away, disappearing into the maze of the hive, but that was not his plan. He stopped to wait for them. His intention was, in fact, to keep them.

Even though he had never been here before, he was able to weave his way through back streets as if he had lived here all his life, as if he had designed them. While guards chased after Djaem, the others moved steadily away, towards the mine's hatch entrance.

The guards pursued Djaem until they all arrived at a guard command center. Djaem had led them there intentionally, as it served the two parts of his plan. The first part, his pursuers watched him enter, creating confusion as they followed. The second part of the plan was the meeting he was scheduled to have.

As Djaem entered, he pulled out his official inspector badge. This gave him a limited measure of authority. He knew this authority fell far short of what he was about to do, but he surmised that the low-ranking desk clerk would not know that. Considering the heavy penalties for disobeying, it was unlikely anyone would take the risk to find out.

"You will direct me to Evers at once," he demanded. "What are you waiting for," he pressed with barely the time to take a breath in between. "Do you want to impede an imperial investigation?"

The look on the poor clerk's face told Djaem of his success even before the frantic clerk replied, "Right away!" Planets have simple crimes and simple penalties. As soon as any issue has imperial attention, it automatically becomes more severe. Most imperial inspectors had a blanket immunity to any crime committed during an investigation. Including unwarranted, cold-blooded murder. Most suspects of imperial investigations would rather die than be brought in. Imperial penalties were always beyond reason. Once convicted, none offered freedom again as long as the convicted shall live. The clerk scrambled to unlock the door to the back rooms as the guardsmen rushed through the front.

"Tell him I'm on my way. And don't delay my team when they arrive."

The pursuing guardsmen stopped as they flooded the office, staring at each other, baffled. Only one guard, a confident officer seeking promotion, followed Djaem down the halls towards the farthest door.

"Stop. Halt! Who are you?" He was ignored and his confidence faltered. "STOP!" This did not happen; Djaem marched quickly to the investigative chief's office.

Djaem had to get his timing just right. As he passed through the opened door and the chief looked up, Djaem turned and addressed the startled man who had been following him. His voice was full of irritation and disdain. "You want me to explain to you why I am here? As an inspector for the Empire, I need to talk to your investigative chief. You want me to explain why you followed me in here? I can't do that. Why don't you give it a try?" Djaem made a waving motion from the guard to the chief.

The guardsman stammered at the surprise confrontation. "We were following you ever since you fled the shooting," he started, trying to find his mental footing.

"The shooting?" Djaem interrupted. "What shooting? Do you mean to tell me you lost a suspect and then came to me for help?" Again, he didn't bother slowing down for an answer. "Or maybe you had no suspect at all, and don't know where to begin? Speak quickly, man, before someone decides that your competence should be investigated."

Blanching and lightly trembling in anger and confusion, the guardsman passed an uncertain gaze to the chief. Djaem cursed under his breath. The chief spoke, "Leave us, Lieutenant. Get a report of your failure ready for my review."

Djaem moved up to the chief's desk as the officer trudged away. A lobby full of guardsmen awaited him with uncertainty. When the lieutenant dropped off the orders to disperse and return to their patrols, the confusion worsened further. Slowly, they filed out. As each patrol group left, the lieutenant met with them, giving them a set of special instructions. By the time he finished, Djaem's team had entered the headquarters, the largest of them, following a blinking tracker.

In the office, Djaem had calmed his breathing. The investigator chief had eyed him with notable suspicion the entire time. Neither spoke for several long minutes. Both were trying to read the other, both trying to plan out the next move. Djaem had to admit, this was the toughest staring contest he had ever been in. Evers was an incredibly competent man.

"Do you know why we are here?" Djaem asked softly. An open question often gets the weak-minded to reveal things, but in this case, it was simply used to gain control of the conversation.

"No. And if you are on business, I should. Speak," Evers countered.

Well. . . that failed miserably. "There have been reports of Ether energies emanating from the mines. Do you have any information on this?" Djaem tried again, this time with a more direct thrust.

"That's really your purpose?" Evers asked, deflecting. "Ether energies. We have a spaceport. Ether energies are common. Probably a stowaway or a ship that washed."

Trying to parry old man? Djaem hid his smile as his recovery from his disadvantage started to take shape. "You weren't listening. It's coming from the mines." He countered as he shook his head. "Nothing made it from the spaceport to the mines on its own without a resounding incident." He pressed his attack.

The inspector smiled, sensing a victory. "Oh, you're interested in the mines? Then that is where your authorization is. If you find anything, let me know. I expect a full report. I'm entitled to a full review before a single word leaves this planet."

Perfect. He's giving orders now. He thinks he is in charge. Djaem beamed inwardly, waiting for Evers to fall into his mental trap. "Yes, of course. You get to look everything over. But you only get to look. Anything relating to the Ether energy in the mines is imperial property." He kept his stance firm to show he wouldn't budge on this point.

BEEEEEEP.

Both men looked at a speaker as it gave a loud alert. That was followed by the clerk's wavering voice. "The other. . . uhh. . . inspectors are here."

"Send them in," the chief ordered. "I want your entire team to know who's in charge here." Djaem simply nodded, hands folded respectfully.

Raza was the first to enter, an arm around the shoulders of the terrified clerk. With a sneer at the chief, she shoved the small clerk back into the corridor just after Uthraith stepped in. Scythia stopped and helped the tiny man back to his feet with a smile before prancing happily into the room.

"Scythia. Manners."

DJAEM SPOKE but two words to her, and all the joy on her face died. She knew he meant she was not to hurt this man, but he rarely used that tone with her. She didn't like it. *I haven't even done anything yet.* Her mouth pressed down into a deep pout. Her shoes clacked loudly as she stomped her feet and sulked to Djaem's left. Her displeasure only grew. She could see their thoughts. She didn't like what she was watching. Not one little bit. They all took a seat in the various chairs.

Evers filled the room. His mind palace burned nearly as brightly as Djaem's, but it was completely different. The shapes and gears were not as elegant. The mental traps were brutal instead of clever. This was a mind built for conquest. His mind was like that of the man that had burned her memories away. Until she had burned him away. The echo of that time rippled through her. It brought back the loss, the anger. Her frustration grew now because Djaem wouldn't let her burn him as she should. Her eyes flashed with heat as she pretended to look down at her shoes, watching the two men in the Ether.

Djaem had drawn most of his thoughts inside himself. He was puny compared to his normal impression in the Ether. Still, where his thought crystals burned, the colors and sounds were sculpted music. Amidst them, something grim lingered. He was guarding his thoughts and letting the brute believe he had won. The brute's fortress was dark and sounded like hammers pounding out a marching beat.

"While you are here, you answer to me. You do not question me. You do not question my men or my orders. Your only jurisdiction is the mine." Inspector Evers rose to his feet in an effort to loom above them. Raza tried unsuccessfully to stifle a chuckle at Evers' expression when he realized that Uthraith was still eye to eye with him. Even seat Uthraith was almost as tall as Evers. The change in his position made Scythia tense, and her hair shifted and fluttered as she tried to control herself.

"And the Ether energy," Djaem added.

"Heh. Still trying to snap up the scraps, are we? Yes, and the Ether energy. That ties to anyone associated with its presence as well. You *will* report to me every second hour. You *will* use these." He pulled four communicator bracelets from his cabinet. With an irritated sound, he reached back in and retrieved four headband lights. "You can use these as well. You will be going into the mines? It would look bad if you turned up dead. My men are not at your disposal. You do your own work, including apprehending any suspects. Is this clear?" He practically snarled as he tossed the items onto the table.

Raza hissed and started to rise but was met by a wave from Djaem. Scythia saw something that made her pout shrink for just a moment. "If it was a stowaway that found its way down, then we'll need to look into the missing children."

"No. The case is closed. If you try to enter the northern district, you will be arrested."

Djaem let his smile show this time. "As you wish. And the spaceport?"

Evers began to look uncomfortable. He thought for a few moments before speaking, his tone now level and well measured. "You have access to the spaceport. But you are not to touch anything without my men present. You are not to pester the freight haulers. You are here for one reason alone: the Ether energy in the mines. If you stray from this in your dealings, you will be jailed." His tone, firm and final.

Smiling broadly, Djaem said, "Very well. We have a lot of work to do." Looking at the others, he said, "Come on. Let's go."

Scythia was the last to leave. She walked out slowly, nodding politely to the inspector. "Sir," she said as the door closed gently behind her, hearing it click. Her hair fluttered as she flexed her will outward. "Stay," she whispered.

Evers's cursing could be heard down the hall. Every mechanical and electrical device in that office bent to her will and stopped working, including the automatic door, which was now locked tight. It would take an arc-welder at least two hours to cut through the bulletproof door.

That ability really is starting to be my favorite! Scythia smiled with deep satisfaction as she skipped to catch up to the others.

"What the hell was that Djaem? You turned us all into lapdogs in there! If you can't handle it, why shouldn't I bleed you myself?" Raza seethed in a whisper, clearly not happy. She grabbed ahold of him in a threatening gesture. It was at this precise moment that a list of profanity beyond Raza's own expertise could be heard from the chief's room. They all stopped long enough to look back. Scythia did her best to look innocent. Lights flickered and went out, then a machine started blasting Djaem with paper. All four of them laughed.

"Good job, Little Blue." Uthraith patted Scythia's head and offered her a candy bar. This was the biggest sweetie she had been given. She beamed with pride, bouncing on her toes. She took her treat eagerly, content to receive it and the praise. She was never as happy as when her little family was happy.

"Not now," Djaem smiled as well but responded to Raza in a serious tone, "or we'll all end up shot. We have to move. Fast."

10

MISSION DAY ONE, ARE WE SCREWED YET?

THE AIR in the actual hive was full of metal and dust. The sounds of massive drills thrummed from the core. A stream of slag workers and ore miners flowed up and down long walkways in and out of the core.

Djaem slowed and turned towards the group. He thought it important to reveal his insight to the others. "He's in on it. The children in cargo crates. He's a part of it." Djaem's voice was low and angry. "He might even be in charge of it. I can't say for sure."

His words came so abruptly that Raza lightly flinched at hearing them. "What, did he tell you that?" she mocked, hoping it was just Djaem's pride speaking. If it were true, it meant a great deal of trouble for her, for all of them.

Djaem snapped back at her. "No, but his lieutenant did. Just, not in as many words. Well, not in any words, but I understood it plain as day. The inspector knows what we did; more importantly, he knows that we know. He will send people after us." He looked up at Uthraith. "Be ready." This brought an excited smile to the giant's face.

Djaem continued, "We found one of their operations

in the core, but there are others. They are primarily working through the northern district but have something set up just east of the spaceport as well."

Scythia frowned as she looked back the way they had come. "There is no greater vengeance than that of mothers." She repeated the quiet whispers she heard in the Ether.

Djaem ran a hand through his hair in agitation. "This is the hive and the mines. No guards are assigned here. It is swarm territory. If you see a uniform, they are hostile. I'll find us a safe place to sleep."

WITH THAT, Djaem dashed into the mild swarm of miners who were gathering to receive their weekly distribution. Scythia watched the mass move as one. She was still amazed at the sameness of all these lights blending and blurring together, connected. She listened to their music, softer here, more placid. Though she found it beautiful, she had a deep understanding that she was not part of it. She was in a tiny boat watching a school of fish flicker through moonlit water.

Uthraith followed the tracker Djaem was wearing. Without it there would be no way to follow him. How do you track a drop of water in the ocean? Scythia skipped along in Uthraith's wake. It kept her from physically touching others. She had figured out how to build her mental armor. She used her memories to define herself. Her pride in recent events helped to hold herself in place. She was a person made of mist, wearing clothes to give herself shape. Even while she hummed the rhythmic pulsing music of the human swarm, she used the link to Djaem to keep the fear at bay. His confidence kept her little boat floating above the surface. The light faded and the buildings closed in over them. They had begun to descend into the core.

The old mine was a honeycomb of older buildings, most still in use. Down the long tunnels was a network of tracks and bridges that had been constructed to transport the ore. As more mines were dug and hollowed out, residences and stores were built in the upper levels. This encouraged the workers to complete the dig as soon as possible. This was one of the first mines completed on the planet; inside was the smelt and refinery so that the ore could be transported off-planet. It was automated. Very few people were needed here. They were used elsewhere. The machines worked tirelessly, smelting and pouring the shiny metal into the molds. That made it easier to load into the storage bins that were then placed onto waiting transport ships.

These walkways were still busy by Scythia's mind, but breathable. The ocean was farther away, but as the buzzing mass receded into the distance, she began to feel it. The eyes watched her, dark and malicious. They were waiting just beyond her sight. She felt the hairs on her neck raise. This wasn't the fear of panic. It was the sense of a predator trying to frighten her. Inwardly she smiled. She would teach it what fear was. Whatever it was would see what she was made of.

WHEN DJAEM SAID that he would find them a place to sleep, he may have been a bit misleading. What he found was a storage container, a purposefully lost or mislabeled one. Someone had paid someone else to lose it in this mine. It was even still partially filled with cargo. The doors of the container were half-covered by some sort of cave-in. Whether it was intentional, or accidental was impossible to tell.

Uthraith had to be the last one in because he barely fit through the opening. Inside was a small dim light that kept the darkness at bay. A makeshift camp had been set up behind the stacked crates. It was purposefully disguised to look like simply spilt cargo. Bedrolls were laid out along with some simple cooking utensils.

"At least it doesn't smell like human waste," Raza said in a sarcastically perky voice.

"It's safe. And defensible. That's what matters," Djaem said quietly.

Scythia stepped in, her shoe clicking loudly and echoing off the metal container. Djaem reached out and touched her arm after two steps. "Scythia, hold on." He knelt in front of her and carefully undid the buckles at her ankles. She used his shoulder for balance as he had her lift her right foot. Carefully, he pulled her foot out of one shoe. Then he repeated the process with the left. Her brow creased as she watched him. Djaem stood up, handing her the shoes. She pouted a little at him. "My feet are cold."

He smirked a bit at her and reached up to pat her head. "It will be fine in a moment."

She nodded and walked quietly into the little camp area. She carried her shoes to the nearest bedroll and sat down, tucking her bare feet under her skirt. All the steel and stone blocked out the Ether. She yawned and rubbed her eyes, blinking sleepily. She was completely unconcerned about the possible dangers. Djaem said it was safe. That was all the reassurance she needed.

Uthraith took up guard at the entrance hole. Looking back, he grinned. "Sleep, Little Blue. Raza, I am hungry."

Raza sighed as she started digging through a pack. She

looked over at Djaem, who was looking through the gear left at the campground and gave him a provocative smile. "We can't forget to feed the monsters now."

Djaem looked at her and gave a smile that showed nothing of how he felt. He knew her smile. She had seen his abilities and was setting her webs, trying to entice him. This was just the first little strand. He needed to be careful.

After a few minutes, Scythia waved at Djaem to get his attention and bring him over. He sat down next to her, and she laid her head down on his lap. She pulled out the doll she had named 'Teddy-bear.'

"In space you can hold on to me. But here I think I need to hold onto you," she whispered low as she shut her eyes. Djaem nodded and worked on sorting out items he had collected from the sorted supplies.

He roused her only once for food. Once she fell back to sleep, he slipped a bedroll under her head so he could take his turn keeping watch. After his watch, he returned to being her pillow. Everyone took shifts keeping watch. Everyone, except Scythia.

Without any discussion, no one woke her for a watch. Maybe because she was dangerous, maybe because she was so childlike. Either way, no one suggested it or wanted it. She slept the deep, restful sleep of someone who had nothing to fear. The others took their four-hour shifts between watching the opening and restless sleep.

SHE WAS STILL HOLDING onto Djaem when he finally woke her softly. To someone who didn't know any differently, it appeared as an affectionate brush of her hair and face. In Djaem's mind he considered it more self-preservation. *When one wakes the beast, it is best to do so with a gentle touch; that way it doesn't bite your hand off.*

It was impossible to tell if it was day or night this far in the core. Scythia's incessant humming was the only sound that marked their passing through the upper tunnels.

Steam rose out of deep crevices, belching up strange gases and smells from underground. The tunnels were narrow passages, walkways over yawning chasms, or tight strips along the sides of massive cliffs that split down into the darkness below. In some tunnels, identified only by nonspecific hazard signs, a faint orange glow could be seen in the depths. They avoided those.

The space between the lights began to grow, forcing them to walk in shadows for longer and longer stretches. Scythia didn't mind the gloom. It put the others on edge. Raza had shivers run along her spine despite the surprising heat of the mines. Uthraith was silent as every instinct urged him to leave this death pit.

The paths were marked by long wires that provided the light to these deeper reaches. On the walls were markings painted by the workers to give direction and warnings. Djaem became increasingly agitated by what they were saying. Warnings of death, pain, and danger. There were other symbols, foul and menacing, that he didn't know.

Each felt it in their own way. The presence, the malignancy in the deep, stalking them just out of sight, waiting in the lightless fissures of rock. Djaem didn't believe in luck. It was simply good planning on his part that they were passing through the pitch-black when Uthraith froze in place.

Uthraith, a natural-born predator, melted into darkness around him, completely silent even with his massive frame. Raza simply cease to exist. Djaem grabbed Scythia, pulling her back to keep her from stepping into the light, his hand covering her mouth. His mind shouted at hers. *Freeze! Quiet; you must be silent! They are coming to get us. They will find us.*

She froze, her eyes wide. She looked for 'they.'

It took her a moment to find their lives in the Ether. Guards. *So many of them.* Twenty-five lives, full of suffering and death. She could feel their intent and more. *Something is wrong. There is something twisting them.* That presence she felt, it was manipulating these souls. Once these guards came into the tunnels, they stopped following orders. She felt their malice, each exponentially rising. They didn't just want to kill them. Blood, violence, pain, suffering, and fear, they wanted all these things.

Uthraith would die fighting. Scythia knew she would be killed as fast as possible, for they feared her power. Djaem and Raza would live for days in these sunless tunnels screaming. Seeing the death they had in store for her Gem caused her fear to rise up inside her chest. She gripped his arm tight as her breathing picked up. What if she couldn't protect her Gem, her spider, and her beast?

Raza's voice whispered from the nothingness. "We can't be cornered here." She had already scouted their surroundings for cover and ambush points; none had been found.

Scythia let her perception extend, and she felt another group coming from other tunnels. The metal and rock kept her perceptions narrow. She whispered against Djaem's hand, "They come from many tunnels."

"They come to their doom." Uthraith growled low and pulled out his axe and his pistol.

Raza whispered softly, "The dark is our ally here. Just be patient and let them come to us. Put her just inside the light, so they will see her. Lure them in and we will be on either side. Uthraith at the end. They will never reach her."

Djaem quickly moved Scythia into position before he took up a position in the tunnel.

Scythia understood her role as bait. Her companions' confidence gave her courage as they took their positions. She flipped on her personal lamp. Her blue skin took on an incandescent glow, her hair a brilliant orange flame. She was a bright and strange candle in the darkness of the tunnel.

She was spotted and the bait quickly taken. They charged her. A man ran forward, trying to close the distance before Scythia realized what was happening. Two men followed close at his heels. At full speed they all ran through the florescent glow cast down from overhead and disappeared into the unlit section. None reappeared in the pool of light on the other side. The few guardsmen farther back slowed down in confusion as Scythia continued to stand unmoved. Four more men failed to reach her before the man with the long rifle in the back decided enough was enough.

She felt his intent as he took aimed at her head. "NO!" she snapped at him, her fear making her angry. The combined force of that anger and fear caused her powers to lash out against him much harder than expected. Even her simple power to break his gun was amplified in these tight tunnels.

The long rifle exploded in his hand. Searing pain filled his face as shrapnel cut through his helmet into his eyes. Blue lightning crackled along the wires, crawling down the tunnels as lights burst in a shower of sparks and fireworks.

Everything plunged into darkness. Shouts echoed through the tunnels.

Raza shouted. "DAMN IT, SCYTHIA! I said we needed to stay in the dark, not MAKE MORE OF IT!"

Uthraith's voice could be heard off to the left. "We

move now. They see in the black; and are running this way. We need to go." The retort of his gun was followed by the unexpected sounds of impact. Even in total darkness, his aim was true. They all turned on their headlamps and started moving down the tunnels. Like little mice in a maze, they twisted and turned. Scythia's lamp had died in the little explosions, forcing her to follow the will-o'-the-wisps created by her team. Her companions were practiced in the art of silence. Scythia might as well have been wearing bells. Her shoes echoed and crunched on the rocks as she ran. Suddenly, Djaem's light began to flicker and fail. Soon, Uthraith's followed. The inspector's instructions about using those headlamps came back to Djaem.

"Fuck, they were sabotaged from the beginning," Djaem whispered to the others.

Raza snorted in disgust as she threw hers off into a chasm. "Well, at least Scythia put us *all* in the dark."

Uthraith sighed and patted Scythia on the head. "She is too loud. They track her noise. Little Blue, you take off the shoes."

"You want her to run through these rocky tunnels barefoot? How will that help? Then, they will just have to track her bloody footprints." There was a faint rustle as Raza shook her head. "No, we can use the noise. It echoes down here. As long as we keep moving and backtracking, they won't be able to pinpoint her."

Djaem agreed. "Yeah, no shoes is not an option down here." When out of his element, Djaem was quick to follow the lead of the more experienced. Scythia didn't bother joining the conversation; she focused on controlling her breathing. Her long legs helped her keep up, but it was hard. Her lungs demanded oxygen, and air was thick here, moist and heavy.

They started running again, the shouts of their

pursuers growing louder than her shoes. Scythia couldn't see in the dark. Instead, she followed Djaem in the Ether. With all the echoes off the rocks she had to block out everything but his lights. She didn't see when Raza and Uthraith turned sharply to head down the tunnel that split off to the left.

DJAEM HAD LIVED his whole life in a crowded hive. He had mastered the air of moving through crowds and disappearing in plain sight. Sneaking in dark wilds was a natural skill for Raza and Uthraith. He followed empty air for two or three minutes before he realized no one was in front of him. It was only because of those loud shoes and swishy skirt that the panic of being alone didn't seize him. He lifted his hand to touch the tunnel wall and kept them moving forward.

THE TUNNELS WERE QUIET, and a faint light could be seen up ahead. Scythia stopped next to Djaem and put a hand on his shoulder. "Raza . . . Uthraith . . . Where?" She was panting and sweating. This was the hardest she had ever run. She liked how her heart pounded, her lungs burned, and her muscles ached. Her physical body was amazing. The fear was secondary to all these new sensations. She knew her Djaem was not as calm.

Djaem didn't seem to know where they were, but as they stood in silence, they could hear far-off screams of men dying. "I think they are okay," he whispered and turned back towards the faint glow.

Scythia nodded and took a moment to calm her

breathing. She faced the glow and understood they had been brought here. "This is it. . . It waits for me." Her whisper floated ominously behind her, and she passed Djaem, walking towards the light.

Djaem grabbed her arm. "Something evil is down there. It could be dangerous. We should wait." He held on tight, trying to pull her back. She shook her head at him.

"It gives the men in the tunnel power, courage, and blood thirst. If we want to help Raza and Uthraith, we have to stop it. Don't worry, Djaem, I will protect you." She smiled and petted him on the head, trying to comfort him. She took his hand and headed towards the light. There wasn't the slightest waver in her step as she entered the large cavern at the end of the tunnel.

11

MISSION DAY ONE: WE ARE DEFINITELY SCREWED

THE STENCH WAS OVERWHELMING. Bits and pieces of decaying bodies decorated the walls. Human skin stretched over openings to other tunnels, trapping the hot, putrid air. The heat was unbearable. There was a pulsing and throbbing from the Ether that even Djaem could feel.

This was a Tyrling Nest.

A pile of mush made up of fat, viscera, and the insides of several people steamed in the center of the cavern. Bones were stacked hap-hazard around the edges of it. Strange, pulsing roots full of blood grew out from the steaming heap of bloody flesh. The mound shifted as if alive.

Every fiber of Djaem's being told him this was death. He should not be here. He should run. He wanted to. However, iron had been infused into his spine. Scythia's madness must have infected his mind because he held his ground, moving in unison with her.

Fuck it. I'm already dead. What's there to lose?

SCYTHIA STEPPED FORWARD as if completely unaware of it all. A voice echoed from some deep place within the cavern, all around them and nowhere at once.

"Pathetic human… tiny psychic. Come to me. I will make you mine." The meat pile shifted and began to grow, throbbing and stretching outward. "I will take my time and enjoy your defilement. I shall rape your mind and consume your flesh. I will absorb your power. We will be one." Grotesque, twisted limbs reached out of the flesh and pushed against the cavern floor. Lifting its black, iridescent body out of the gushy, slimy bed of death, it was twisted and vaguely humanoid, constructed from those it had collected. "You are strong. This will make me strong. I will drink the blood of your friends and then this hive will be. . ."

Scythia's eyes narrowed in anger as the voice threatened Djaem. She brought a finger to her lips, and her voice echoed her mind.

"SHUSH!" she commanded. It was the motion of her fingers, a stomp of her foot. It was the equivalent of putting her will into motion.

The beast felt an unbearable pressure. In an instant, it realized its terrible mistake. For her will was that of a newborn star, bending the universe around her. Her gravity pulled everything towards that burning light. The demon could no longer speak. It crumpled to its many knees before her.

DJAEM WATCHED with awe and horror at his beautiful blue monster. Her clicky shoes squished in the refuse beneath her feet. Her skirt swished, barely out of reach of the coagulated blood and gore. She watched the repulsive thing writhe and snarl as it was bent at her feet. She stepped forward slowly. Djaem recognized Raza's expression of disgust as it crossed Scythia's face. She lifted her foot and pressed her heel down on the creature's back. It flopped and frantically struggled to get away. She didn't see the man coming out from behind the sinew curtain. He was wrapped in robes of black.

The light off the edge of the blade flashed as the man aimed at Scythia's back. The heavy thump was followed by a red splatter and the knife landing on the floor. Djaem's small dagger was buried deep in the man's right eye. Djaem stared at the Demon-keeper's dead body. *Stupid fool. You should have fled when you saw that my monster was stronger than yours. Why would you risk your life for your monster?*

In an excellent impersonation of Uthraith, Scythia smiled and ran a long blue finger over the delicate horns that ridged and weaved into a lace made of bone on the Tyrling's brow.

"I think I would like a hat," she whispered. Scythia twitched her head to the side; with a horrific gurgling crunch, her power crushed the beast. Djaem flinched back at the sound, his eyes wide. The only thing left of the creature was the head; the rest rejoined the pile of gore in which it slept. Splashes of glowing blue ichor sprayed against her skirt and shoes as she pulled the head free. Lifting it up in her hands, she grinned, pleased with herself. It had taken as much effort to kill the beast as it had for Djaem to throw his knife or run through a crowd.

Djaem tried to understand what had just occurred. This demon—this beast from another world that could have gained enough power to kill every living soul in this hive—was gone with a twitch of her head. A shiver ran along his spine. His monster was indeed more dangerous than he realized. He had to keep her under control.

Djaem frowned as he watched her display with the demon's skull. He didn't think it was good that she had picked up so many habits from his fellows. *She is filling in her gaps with pieces of us.* He would have to talk to her about that. Later… if they ever made it out of this hole.

SCYTHIA LOOKED at the creature's head with a frown. Uthraith carried trophies from those he had defeated. She didn't have a head bag, and it was dripping all over the place. She remembered that Uthraith said heat was the key. She concentrated her flame on the skull. The process looked very different between the Ether and the real world.

TO DJAEM, Scythia's hand suddenly burst into blue flames with orange jets, a burning version of her skin and hair. It consumed the Tyrling's head and cooked off the blood and skin. Djaem was sure it would have smelled atrocious if the stink of the place hadn't been so horrific already. It only took a minute of this high-intensity flame to clean the skull to the bone. She placed it on her head. Oddly enough, the skull fit just over the crown of her head, fitting so that she could look out the front nostrils as if they were eye holes.

A hysterical laugh escaped Djaem. The sight of her was horrific yet childish. He managed to get a hold of himself and motioned her back out the door. He could hear shouts and footfalls.

"Scythia, dearest, can you shield us from bullets?" he asked as she headed toward the exit.

She shook her head. "I don't think so. I don't really move things with my mind. Anytime I try to concentrate on something like that, they burst into flames."

Flaming bullets! We'll have to try that sometime, on someone else. She took his hand and followed him back out the cavern entrance into the dark. *Why don't I burst into flames, then?*

They ran along the path back until Scythia tripped over a dead man. His head had been completely twisted around; his little head lamp gave a ghastly display of his back. Scythia snatched up his light along with his pistol. Djaem searched for another body, taking his gear as well. In one hand he held the pilfered pistol; with the other he gripped Scythia's hand tightly. They took off again without making a sound.

Djaem suddenly became aware of her noiseless steps. He slowed as he looked back at her to see she was floating just a few inches off the ground. In the dark it was hard to see the side effects of her Ether powers. He stopped and took a moment to look. He realized the walls were oozing blood, and the air was colder than it had been. He was grateful for the dark.

Screams and shouts echoed madly down the tunnels. Djaem was so focused on chasing the sounds that when Uthraith appeared out of the inky black, Djaem fired the pistol. The bullet pinged uselessly off the stone at Uthraith's side. It ricocheted, almost hitting Scythia. She didn't notice and continued panting heavily from all the running.

Uthraith shook his head like a disappointed father. He crossed his arms over his massive chest. "Training. Both of you."

Raza frowned as she approached and looked at Scythia's head. "That is a category two Tyrling! One of those completely wiped out Durmount," she said in a furious whisper.

Scythia tilted her head to one side. "What is Durmount?" she asked in a breathless whisper. Raza groaned and seemed to try to gather patience. "Doesn't matter; why is it on your head," she said with controlled calm.

Scythia smiled brightly and straight it with pride. "It's my new hat." Raza gaped at her and then snapped a look at Djaem as if it were his fault.

Djaem just shrugged in response. "You tell her she can't have it."

Uthraith tilted his head as he considered the skull. "Hmm, good start. Will teach how to decorate. Make it pretty hat."

Scythia nodded and beamed with joy.

THE PACE of their trek out of the mines was just short of a run. Djaem was no good at pacing; he was a sprinter. Raza, who took the lead, said they should avoid stopping to rest "every two minutes." Scythia's long legs helped, but she had trouble keeping up.

Uthraith would run ahead of the group or break off to one side or another. Oddly, these departures were rarely followed by the type of battle sounds one would expect. Occasionally, there would be a single shot fired. Most often there was silence. The horrible screaming would begin shortly after he had returned to the group.

Truly a man of horrific talents, mused Djaem to himself.

When they approached the hatch back into the city core, Djaem asked that Uthraith and Raza slow down.

"Give us sixty paces," he said.

"Sixty?" Uthraith questioned, looking at a distant stone wall.

Djaem groaned and palmed his face in irritation. "Ugh. I mean sixty HUMAN paces! Sixty of my steps, alright? I will go ahead sixty steps first."

The giant smiled at him. It was hard to tell if he was teasing or not. Growing up in a barren frontier world taught Uthraith's people how to use long strides to conserve energy. His step was almost twice Djaem's.

There were soldiers at the gate, just as he expected. Djaem did not need to speak a word before Raza cursed under her breath, "Fucking bloodbath." He was relieved she already saw what was about to happen. *The more in-tune we are for this, the better it will be for everybody. Well. . . everybody except the guardsmen.* He motioned for Scythia to stay back.

Unlike before, Djaem led the way with his badge out. Raza walked calmly beside him. The inspector snarled at Djaem's approach. "Halt, you are to stay down there. Your assignment does not excuse the murder of my men."

The words would have removed any doubt that Djaem was the enemy, if they had the time to sink in.

Even Uthraith had trouble following what happened next. Raza cut the captain's arm with her blade, and as he flinched, Djaem delivered a finishing stab with his own. They moved like dance partners, spinning and twirling around each other as if they had performed this act a dozen times. They each had dispatched one of the captain's soldiers before the rest even realized there was an attack.

The numbers were on the side of the two-blade wielders. The soldiers had automatic weapons, but the tunnels were narrow. They couldn't to open fire without hitting each other. Their body armor was made to protect against gunfire but made them slow. The blades fit easily into the softer joints and between the plates.

The two handlers had learned each other's moves well. Every maneuver looked so well coordinated with the next, a choreographer could not have designed it better. Every gun that was brought to bear against one of the bladed terrors was met by a knife from the other. Every thrust at a defending soldier was a ploy to move them into the reach of the real attacker. Killing is not a beautiful act. However, at this moment, the dance of death they performed came close. The blades hit their marks, and blood poured from wounds. They fell quickly but death would be slow to claim them.

Uthraith, who had started to charge, slowed himself. His face was overtaken by a massive smile. "She is magnificent," he said quietly to no one in particular. He pulled out his rifle and waited for the tide to turn. He didn't interfere but was ready. Anyone could make a mistake, and the advantage of the two he called friends declined along with the number of guardsmen.

SCYTHIA SAW A DIFFERENT PICTURE. The mindlights of her friends joined together in a way she had never seen. Even when Djaem played his game on others, it was not like this. Their lights and crystals bounced and reflected back and forth like infinity mirrors. He also danced his mind amongst the soldiers, much the same way he did the men on the ship. Djaem knew their feelings and intentions. He could guess which ones would try to shoot and which ones were too scared. He then could share that information with Raza with just a twist or position of his body.

Scythia could also see the other side of it. Fear and agony and loss started pouring out from the scene before her. It was painful, almost unbearable. When she couldn't take it anymore, she reached out and touched the light that was flowing between Djaem and Raza. The dance of their minds would be the key to ending the dance of pain. She simply pushed it. The light became less a manifestation of their thoughts and ignited into a real, physical fire. Raza and Djaem shouted, jumping back to avoid the sudden burst of flames. They immediately fled the area.

Tears streamed out of Scythia's eyes as she intensified the heat. The mercy that fueled the fire made it burn all the hotter. Within a few heartbeats, there was little aside from helmets that could still be identified. Uthraith smiled softly and put away his rifle. He rested an enormous hand on her head.

"That is enough, Little Blue."

ONCE INSIDE THE CITY CENTER, Raza and Djaem had a long discussion. They knew the inspector chief was not going to let them off this planet alive after what they had discovered. Finding a way to get all of them off-world without causing too much destruction would be a near impossible task. So, it took them ten minutes to work out their plan.

Raza was an expert in concealment and would lead the others on short hops without being detected. Djaem had established a rapport and understanding with several residents in their short meetings. Word had spread quickly about the group rescuing the local children. They coordinated a path of houses that were believed friendly to make it to the spaceport. Once there, they would fall under full imperial protections again. There were enough imperial guards to ensure their safety.

If they got there, they could take the transports off-world. Once in space, they were home free. The inspector could piss and moan all he wanted but reporting any of this would only bring more investigators to his planet. If he had one dirty secret, that meant he had others. He wouldn't want them to be found.

"The inspector didn't call forth a Tyrling," Scythia said finally. She didn't know or care if anyone was listening. Nor did she care if she was interrupting them. Her mind buzzed with its own thoughts. She held up her new hat and inspected it.

"This was a fully grown, fully powered Tyrling. It was being controlled. It wanted to run wild and consume every-one, but it was bound. That would take a very powerful mind." Her frown deepened as she tilted her head. She let out a frustrated sound. "But I don't feel any other psychics. Maybe they are gone now."

Even if Djaem did believe in luck, he certainly didn't believe they were lucky enough for that to be true. Raza and Djaem exchanged a worried look as they considered the implications.

Uthraith smiled and lifted the skull of the Tyrling, "There are few men in my tribe that have faced these crea-tures. Fewer still who have trophies." He grinned. "I am not worried about who bound this weak creature." He affectionately stroked Scythia's flaming hair. "Our Little Blue is stronger."

Scythia scrunched up her face in a beaming smile, her cheeks blushing at the high praise. Djaem was once again faced with the realization that treating her as a favorite pet was NOT the wisest of plans. Raza nodded. She wasn't worried about some unknown psychic. She was worried about their own. *She took it on by herself, without a scratch. How. . .*

Djaem worried about Scythia for a completely different reason. He was concerned about what damage she would do if she lost control in that crowd again. *I don't want half the hive to die in writhing agony.*

12

MISSION DAY TWO: HOW ARE WE NOT DEAD YET?

SCYTHIA HAD no idea what was going on. She was beginning to worry about Djaem and Raza. They made her wear this weird shawl over her head and around her face. It covered her new hat and kept her hair tucked away. She didn't get to wear her clicky shoes. She was upset about that until Djaem gave her these little sandals that scuffed in the dirt. They had little tassels on the end that were fun to swing.

Raza was leading them through a maze of passageways. They were made of tunnels and cargo containers. Many were so short; Scythia had to crouch or crawl through. Scythia was amazed at how long and far Uthraith was able to walk crouching. Her legs burned and her back ached. The clothes she was wearing made her sweat. She disliked it very much.

She didn't complain, however, because she got to meet so many new people. She was most excited when she met the children. They were pretty little lights. Their minds were so free in comparison to those of adults.

The team would walk a wandering path and then slip into some crowded box where Scythia would sit off to one side and play with the children. There were so many. They would crawl on her and touch her face and hair. She met a set of twin boys that used the Ether to talk to each other. They told her all about how happy they were, how they loved their mother and father. They showed her their favorite memories and thoughts. She got to feed them and sing with them. They were so tiny she could hold them both at the same time. They were only two cycles old. The family of twins had many children.

DJAEM WAS a bundle of nerves when Scythia first played with the children. *Apparently, maternal instincts are not stored in the memory.* He realized that her finding those kids was not a fluke. This was at the core of who she was. This was natural to her. *While she is sitting with them, those children are the safest beings on this planet.*

RAZA WATCHED Scythia with the twins, with both amusement and concern. "Let's hope she doesn't want to take one home," she whispered to Djaem. As the words left her, an unwelcome thought came to her. *What if she had her own baby somewhere?* Raza felt the stinging bite of empathy for Scythia in that moment. If Scythia had a child, it would have been killed when she was taken. It was unlikely any trace of her past life remained. *It's better this way. It's better to forget that kind of pain.*

Uthraith was not surprised by Scythia's behavior. He

encouraged her to play with the children. They belonged in the same group as far as he was concerned. *Like should be with like.*

THE FAMILY'S ELDEST SON, Kreck, had been missing for days. The boy had been in a cargo crate, minutes from being shipped off-world. Scythia recalled he was the second to last crate she had opened. His mother could barely stop weeping with gratitude. The family had piled on top of her, hugging and crying. Scythia was surprised how good it felt. The difference between this and what happened in the street was that it felt like she was part of the group, not erased by it.

Kreck was on the cusp of adulthood, so he tried hard not to cry. Scythia smiled at him and hugged him tightly, petting his hair affectionately. The youth turned several shades of red but didn't complain. The hardest part was leaving, but eventually Scythia reluctantly returned the children and said her goodbyes. She reached in her pocket and pulled out a handful of money chits, putting them on the table.

Raza and Djaem stared at her in surprise. Raza whispered to Djaem, "When did she get that?"

Djaem shrugged, confused. "Why did she get it? When did you learn about money, Scythia?"

Scythia smiled and hugged the mother one more time. "It was in the data crystals you gave me."

Just before they stepped out of their cube, she paused and reached into the Ether. She shifted her vision and moved the energies, changing their flow to bring life and vitality. At that moment everyone in this area was in near perfect health. This cured any disease they may have contracted and removed any injury that had been plaguing them. She was not powerful enough to make the flow last, but it did allow them to start from a healthy place. This was the happiest thing she had experienced so far. She would cherish this new memory she had made.

THIS HIDING and scurrying plan worked well. The path ended less than half a sector away from the spaceport docks. Unfortunately for the team they had a problem. The inspector knew a thing or two about chasing rats in the tunnels. He decided to set his trap at the exit and flush them out from the other end. He knew the undisputable fact; there was only one spaceport on this planet. They would have to go there eventually. He had deployed two full battle companies to the sector. Raza and Djaem had expected that. It was his other actions they had not.

He had closed outbound crafts and shut down the automated shuttles carrying ore. Every hour he would lose a great deal of money. Raza and Djaem had underestimated how much he was willing to lose to catch them.

The people of the hive were neither blind nor dumb. The story of the Star-born rescuing the children had spread like fire through dry kindling. It grew with every retelling. By the time Scythia reached the end of their path, rumors had her rescuing hundreds of children and fighting entire combat units.

Heavily armored soldiers were posted at every intersection. The hive was angry and restless. The sight of these men abusing their power did not go unnoticed by the people who lived there. Scythia felt uneasy; the rise in discontentment prickled her skin. Djaem squeezed Scythia's shoulder to help her calm down.

"Don't worry, dear. I have a plan," he whispered in her ear. He spoke quietly to the entire group. He made each one promise to follow the plan exactly, no matter what happened to him. Scythia could see a little bit of deception flitting about him in the Ether. His words were changing as they went to Raza, hers did the same to him. They were holding a private conversation right in front of her and Uthraith.

She trusted him completely. Otherwise, this would have bothered her quite a bit. She liked having him all to herself.

"Stay here for exactly twelve minutes, and then go," he repeated. "I will distract the guards. You just keep moving. Use the disguises, but don't worry about hiding yourselves. We are almost there." He slid the filthy clothes on over his own and made his way out to the streets. Upset citizens were already arguing with soldiers.

Scythia touched the head wrap and looked at Raza and Uthraith. "I must keep wearing this and walk to the ship," she repeated her instructions carefully. Raza smiled and nodded. "Yep, easy as you please. Like a stroll through a garden."

DJAEM TRIED a few hot buttons first. He called out how his cousin was missing, and the guardsmen refused to act. He commented on the full rations they received while working families starved. It worked to rile people up, but not enough. These guards were in heavy armor and carried guns to match. Mentally, Djaem counted every passing second. *One-nineteen, two minutes.*

Next, he moved on to the soldiers. He used the echoes and their armor to say things that the crowd wouldn't hear. "My kid's gone. . . find him and maybe you'll find yours." While this got some reaction, "Thank the gods the inspectors gave us these" was much more effective. The soldiers became edgy and aggressive. His distraction was perfectly on track. He just needed to push both sides a little more. *Three-ten, three-eleven. . .*

He began to shift the crowd towards the intersection with the disbursement center. To the people, he edged them on with rumors of a food shortage in order to supply the extra guards. He made his way to the edge of the crowd and then drew in the crowd, making himself the new center. It didn't take much for the Hive-born; they shifted this way naturally. This made people like Djaem extraordinarily rare and exceptionally dangerous in these crowds. They were the herd hounds amidst the sheep. Here he had an army of angry restless ants.

Soldiers tried to keep their distance, exactly as Djaem had anticipated. It was going perfectly to plan all the pieces moving as he wanted.

That all changed with the arrival of Inspector Evers himself. "Idiots," he barked at the soldiers. "He's here. In the crowd! The short one. . . with the. . . well, from my office!" As angry as Evers was, even he couldn't recall Djaem's features.

Djaem's elusively plain face had served him once again. However, his troubles were becoming severe, and his situation, desperate. *Four-fifty-one, four-fifty-two, four-fifty-three.*

He needed to make it to the second intersection before the others stepped out. The entire plan hinged on this timing. The arrival of Inspector Evers threw a wrench in his plans. At the inspector's command, the soldiers stopped keeping their distance from the Hive-men. They spread out to block the advance and readied shock-sticks. A thinner second rank prepared rifles. The crowd was once again uncertain. Fear and anxiety filled the air. *Five-eighteen. . . five-nineteen, c'mon!*

Desperate times call for desperate measures. Djaem approached the inspector. "You ain't even from here, grayback! We just want our food. We still gettin' our shares today, right?" He looked the inspector square in the eyes.

The inspector glared back with fiery intensity. "You will get what I give you!" His angry barking drew an angry rumble from the crowd. He looked around and his annoyance intensified. "I know you. I recognize those eyes. . ." The inspector fought inside his own mind trying to place the face. "You! You're that troublemaker from shaft two, aren't you?"

Djaem had to fight the laugh but knew this was a small victory. Wearing the thick-soled boots had paid off, but his time was running out. The inspector stepped quickly behind a pair of advancing soldiers who reached to seize Djaem. He jerked himself back into the crowd and stumbled over a rock. *Five-ninety. . . five-nine*—His count ended abruptly as a door behind him burst open. Three shrouded figures sprinted to the side street as Djaem had instructed.

"Damn it! They're early!" he cursed out loud. He saw only one option. Violence.

Grabbing the rock he had tripped on, he rose quickly. He cast it as part of an exaggerated hand gesture while barking out, "You're making shit up!" The rock, intended for a second-row guard armed with a rifle, was meant to cause an accidental trigger. The swarm would stampede, and the path would be opened. If Djaem believed in luck, it would only be in bad luck.

Again, he watched his plan fall moments short, and

again, it was the fault of the inspector. The tall man spun around in a military-style reverse step. His mouth opened to speak when the rock struck him. Surprise and pain sent him to the ground.

"It's them!" One of his lieutenants shouted, pointing to the escaping figures, but the inspector could not respond.

The crowd fell silent in shock, not knowing where the attack on the inspector came from. This silence ended abruptly as the line of soldiers started applying their shock-sticks in defense of their commanding officer. As the first hiver screamed in pain, the dam burst. The crowd responded in kind. They swarmed the line and tried to overbear their attackers.

The inspector's senses returned amidst this chaos. "No! Men, stop! It's him!"

The noise of the swarm when calm can be deafening. When riled into a frenzy and backed by fighting, it is nearly impenetrable. The lieutenant continued trying to get the inspector's attention. This was the last threat to Djaem's plan.

Stepping between the two men, Djaem pulled back his hood looking Evers in the eye.

"Here's your report," he grinned manically and tossed the papers directly overhead. The lieutenant dashed to grab him, but Djaem was long gone before the first paper hit the ground.

Grabbing the lieutenant's arm, Evers commanded, "Get him!" He pointed after Djaem. The lieutenant protested and tried pointing out the other hooded figures, but Evers insisted. Soon, Djaem had a dozen soldiers trying to navigate a violent stinging swarm in pursuit of him.

At the next intersection, when the three shrouded

figures emerged, Djaem yelled, "Container. Western quad!" His voice somehow carrying over the noise of the mob. The shortest of the three nodded and ran ahead. *Chaos and confusion can be the greatest weapon, in the right hands.* Djaem started moving again with a smile.

13

MISSION DAY TWO: SO MUCH FOR THE PLAN

DJAEM RAN for five minutes before arriving at the spaceport. Even though he did not have the trouble of navigating the swarm the others did, he was out of breath. He immediately headed to Artos's office. When he pushed the outside button, the door whooshed up. Djaem was immediately unnerved and ducked into a group of nearby people.

Artos wouldn't leave the door unlocked. This should have simply rung a buzzer. Two guardsmen slowly peeked out of the open door. The one on the left shrugged and they returned inside. The door closed again. He had barely escaped that ambush.

A sense of deep dread rose in Djaem. His mind danced over what had transpired. First there was, the Inspector Chief Evers with his heavy-handed use of power—that behavior was rare for someone who already had all the power. *He was a top dog but still on someone else's leash.* Then Artos had reported himself as a simple guardsman. Artos acted as if his authority didn't extend past the spaceport. Djaem suddenly recalled that Artos had activated the screens without a hand or a voice command. The office was full of suppressors. Artos had tried to give them information on the Tyrling but had been upset when they had already found it. Dread seized Djaem.

He was right there all along. I let the real monster slip through my fingers.

Frantically, he scanned the spaceport. Their own shuttle was intact but surrounded by imperial guardsmen. A large group of soldiers were busy evacuating the spaceport for 'security.' Another group headed into the western district following the hooded decoys. Djaem radioed Raza.

Raza, Uthraith and Scythia had been following behind a mass of rioting Hive-men and the collection of guards. Djaem had spent exactly ten minutes setting the scene, and Raza made sure everyone stayed put for the entire twelve minutes. By then the soldiers had cleared a path the team could move along. The soldiers were dealing with the people in front of them; they never once looked back.

"I. . . I'm sorry. I fucked up. Bad. I'm not sure if I can fix this one. He. . . he got me. He got me good. Listen, I need you to help them evacuate the port. I have a new plan." His voice was a heavy anxious whisper.

Uthraith's laugh boomed over the radio. "Su-qua! I never thought I would hear those words from you!"

Raza's voice followed, clearly snatching the radio from Uthraith. "We're coming up on it now, but I'm not sure how we can get everyone out of here. There's still too many soldiers, and if they spot us, they'll bring the whole contingent back."

SCYTHIA SMILED, glad to finally be able to help. "I can do it," she said in a soft voice. She did not wait for a response. She walked calmly into the spaceport. The few unfortunate enough to spot her immediately doubled over and collapsed. They felt as if their bones were being flattened. Their screams were excellent motivators for the evacuation.

FAR ABOVE, now on the catwalk, Djaem continued searching for Artos or his shuttle. He found it, because it was the only one currently being loaded. Small crates with green and yellow crystal symbols were being carried onboard, but Artos himself was nowhere to be seen.

Were he a decent shot, Djaem could have disrupted the loading by sniping one of the men. Had he known more about spacecraft, he could have isolated the launch field. Unfortunately, these were things Djaem knew were not options because of his own shortcomings. Looking around, he saw his only solution. He rushed frantically along the catwalk, heading to the command tower.

As he ran, a woman's voice, too loud in volume to be as soft and kind as it was in tone, filled the air above the spaceport. "We are with Special Division. I need you to leave the spaceport. I need you to go now, find safety. Please go home to your families now."

Scythia was gentle with her will making it a request instead of a demand. They heeded Scythia's voice. Even Djaem started to look for an exit before he remembered… he has no surviving family, and his home was a galaxy away. He shook her voice out of his head and finished his climb to the tower. The lone guardsman was in a panic. He fled without a fight. Djaem was grateful. He wasn't sure it was a fight he would have won.

Slipping into the control chair, he looked over the shuttle list. It wasn't long before he found the one, he was after. An automated refueling shuttle was waiting, inbound after using half its load. *This will do perfectly.* He could not adjust the controls; he did not know how they worked. He did, however, know the navigation system.

He restarted the automated system. Then he did what he does best. He lied. He told it that the bay it needed to dock in was two hundred feet lower than it really was and a thousand feet to the west. These coordinates placed it about twenty feet below Artos's shuttle.

People were fleeing from the spaceport at a record pace. It was understandable, considering that every guard within a hundred feet of a blue-skinned, flame-haired Starborn woman was writhing and screaming in agony. Even the members of the swarm helped the guardsmen flee. All carried word back with them.

Djaem slid down the ladder to the ground floor. As his feet touched the floor, he noticed that Scythia was not moving. She stood unmoving, repeating her message to go home right now. Djaem started in her direction when she added a few extra words. "I will be alright. I am a friend of flame. Fire will not hurt me."

Djaem needed no further urging. He wasn't sure if a psychic could protect themselves from such a blast. However, if he had learned anything on this mission, it was that Scythia was stronger than anyone knew. He ran all the way to Artos's office. The two guardsmen worried him, but a tiny laugh of relief escaped him as he saw them writhing on the ground in front of the office. Dragging the two men through the door, he engaged the lockdown. When the blast doors fell and suppressors came on, the two guardsmen were released from their agony. Djaem blanched, staring at them as they rose shakily to their feet.

One of them took a seat at Artos's desk, the other across the room. "Not sure what you saved us from," one said, "but thanks." The guards looked at each other. They were very much in agreement: they didn't get paid enough for this.

Djaem smiled and nodded. "Don't mention it." *And thanks for not doing me in.*

THE ENTIRE COLONY shook with the impact and subsequent explosion. Two shuttles with their power cores and half a pay load of fuel were involved. Fire suppression systems kicked in. Alarms blared and safety measures went into overdrive. Sensors in the office told Djaem when it was safe to leave.

"All clear," he radioed to the others.

"Do I even want to know what in the name of the Powers you just did?" Raza hissed. "We're gonna be a minute. The passage collapsed. Finding a different route."

Djaem headed out the door. Outside the office, some fires still burned. Tiny robots flitted about applying suppressants. Unmoved from her original spot, Scythia stood at the very center of the spaceport. His relief that she appeared unharmed was buried beneath his agoraphobia. The spaceport was completely empty. It was a mile wide and half that long. Their tiny shuttle was all the way at the far end. He felt his strength dwindling and his hands began to shake. His heart pounded in his chest and his breathing came in tight gasps. Slowly, one step at a time, he started in the direction of their shuttle. The soldiers would be here before too long. Now was the time to escape.

He knew what he needed to do. Crossing the spaceport meant survival. Simple. He knew he could do it without harm. Most of the spaceport was free of flames. However, this place should have half a million people in it. Instead, it had only one. His feet stopped moving. The fear was intense; it overrode all his other fears, even the demand for escape. It overcame his sense of duty to get the information off-world. It even surpassed his need to survive. Angry tears glistened in his eyes as he struggled. His muscles tightened and his throat constricted, making it hard to breathe. His heart hammered and skipped in his chest; the taste of copper filled his mouth. He hated himself at that moment. He could not do this alone. His only option was to wait for the others to arrive. His eyes went to Scythia's and her strange, childlike movements. The sight of her brought some slight comfort to him. *What is she doing?*

FLAMES DANCED with Scythia and she with them. Wisps of it flitted about her, both in the Here and in the Ether. She enjoyed the dance and spoke with the inferno as only she could. It spoke back, sharing with her the secrets of how it existed in both worlds at once. She returned a similar tale of herself. She drew the fire inward, holding it close.

She whispered to embers like a lover, friend, mother, and daughter. She was all these things at that moment. Keeping the blaze contained intensified the heat, melting what used to be writhing men into nothing more than permanently smudges in the rock. However, the heat did not spread, protecting the children she had saved, keeping the hive from burning. Enveloped in the Ether and standing by the flames, Scythia never saw him.

SHE COULDN'T SEE ARTOS. His suit was specially designed to mask him. It shielded him from weapons, fire, space, and even the sight of those who used the Ether.

Artos walked slowly through the real fire and the Ether fire. He had no fear of the Star-born psychic. His suit would protect against pyrokinesis and mind control, as well as physical attacks from any blaster she might have. His weapon was a massive sword designed to channel his own psychic energy. He lifted his long blade, coming up behind the bizarre woman.

Why did they say she was so powerful? So, what if she could control fire? Many psychics could do that.

The crystals set along the edge of the blade began to glow a sickly green and then shifted to orange as his telekinetic strength assisted the blade's movement. With the start of his swing, the crystals on his armor flashed to the same eerie shine. The blade came down but had been knocked wide of the intended target, wounding instead of killing.

THE LAST FEW moments flashed through Djaem's mind as he lay on the ground, the pain of a broken collarbone informing him of his stupid mistake. He saw the man in the powered armor come up behind Scythia through the fire. He knew there was no way to warn her. She was too deeply immersed in the Ether to see the physical world. His body had moved without any hesitation. His legs raced towards her. Using the avoidance methods, he had seen Raza use, he circled around a set of flames to come up on Artos's blind side. Moving at a full sprint, he charged and dove into the backside of the man's braced knee.

Djaem's mental calculations concluded that with the weight of the armor, the acceleration of the sword pushing in one direction, coupled with the exertion of Djaem's mass at full speed, Artos's knee would snap like a twig. He was wrong. Instead, it was Djaem who broke, bent around the armored leg. One inch of space and a translucent glow separated the two men.

Once Djaem had run into steel support pillars in his youth. They were more forgiving. The telekinetic field enveloping this man's armor was something Djaem had never heard of.

"Worthless flea!" Artos made a dismissive gesture at him, then turned to pull his sword out of the reinforced endurium deck plates. With that gesture, Djaem was struck by nothing less than a wrecking ball, and he was flung into the air. He instantly knew at least one rib was broken from the initial impact and suspected it was worse than that. His self-assessment was interrupted by his body's rapid return to the ground. The impact snapped the humerus and ulna of his left arm and finished off at least one more of his bruised ribs. The rib that was initially broken worked its way into something inside him. Djaem tried to glance down, but darkness closed in around his vision, which had become fixated on the now protruding collarbone.

SCYTHIA'S ATTENTION snapped from the flame as she felt a surge. *My Gem!* She felt his pain, and a new emotion flooded its way into her understanding. Rage. Her pain was dim, distant, a whisper to the howl of Djaem's agony.

The walls wept tears of blood as all the flames pushed into the Ether. Her feet lifted off the deck plates, which started to boil where she once stood. Artos barely managed to free his sword when her rage found its target. For the first time in her known existence, she had to push on the Ether. She cried out, lifting her arms to press harder. She struggled, using all her strength. Every fiber of will she possessed went into trying to end this fiend. Her mind was frantic and spinning in rage and fear. *He hurt Djaem. Djaem's hurt. . . AND HE DID IT!*

FEW WOULD REFER to the energy that manifested on top of Artos as flames. It was a column of white golden heat, so intense that flames could not exist in it lest they be burned away. He shifted his sword from striking posture to shielding his face instead. Several of the crystals on his armor cracked and shattered. Burn welts began to rise on Artos's skin. He, too, learned a new emotion that day. Fear.

He had been so confident in his great psychic power, the power of the crystals, and the strength of his armor. Nothing had the power to reach him, he was untouchable. He was unkillable, maybe even immortal. He had all the time in the world. Suddenly faced with the real possibility of his demise, Artos saw the need for the utmost urgency.

Both Artos and Scythia had failed to face true foes before. They had grown arrogant in their powers. Now both felt the fear that accompanied a true test of their strength.

The very air around them crackled and whipped with the force of their power. The Ether was a maelstrom of energy, will pressing against will. Even the monsters in the Ether moved away. The hurricane of damage caused by their battle would scar the Ether for ages to come. Only a fraction of this battle of titans was felt in the physical world, leaving paranormal echoes behind. The stones would whisper their thoughts out loud. Items would slide, drawn to the spot of the battle. An unusual cold or hot spot would make its way into the spaceport. All these things would remind future generations of what took place here.

Artos shifted his focus in the Ether to suppressing her ability to shield herself as he stepped back with one leg. This movement pivoted him, allowing him to point the tip of his guarding blade at Scythia's throat. As he began to thrust forward, the solar flame encircling him vanished. It ended, and new pain pierced his body, the left shoulder, to be precise.

The force of the thrust was enough to bend and snap Djaem's dagger once it had been penetrated between the armor plates. The razor-sharp blade wounded Artos's immortal body. Even in this frenzy, Scythia had to protect her Djaem from blazing heat. The flame was released, not quenched. The blade fell from Artos's hands as the force of his own strength tore at his flesh. One metal hand grabbed the source of this new wound. He searched for the fool that dared attack him.

It was the same verminous flea he swatted moments earlier. Djaem had found the strength to sacrifice himself a second time. Turning on Djaem, Artos focused his tele-kinetic strength on Djaem's very bones. Artos grabbed Djaem, lifting him in the air with a gauntleted fist. *Tearing you apart from the inside will rid me of this pest for certain.*

"Listen, flea! You may have bit my dog but know that I am the master!" His monologue was cut short by smooth, dulcet, and deadly feminine tones from behind him. The very Ether quaked with her fear and fury. Scythia's scream could be heard three stars away. All the heat of the sun could not stop the shiver that ran along Artos's soul. He was a fool. He had let the flea and his pride distract him.

"His name is Djaem. Now, you burn." Hers was the last voice he would ever hear. The agony from within was so great he could not listen to his own screams. His pain could be felt far beyond the echo of her scream.

SCYTHIA HAD SEEN she could not burn through his armor, but she had learned two very important lessons. The first was that the flames can exist in the Here, in the Ether, or both. The second was that, if Artos's telekinesis could manifest inside Djaem, then her flame could manifest inside Artos. She pulled in every ember, every cinder, and every flicker. She poured everything she could into this flame; never had she reached her limits before. She rammed against the edges of herself as hard as she could.

Blood gushed from her nose as she was forced out of the Ether, no longer able to hold herself there. With every bit of her power drained, she collapsed in a heap. Beneath her the charred, melted glass and metal changed color as her blood seeped and spread out. The hissing sizzle of it was lost in the noise.

In the delirium caused by his wounds and internal bleeding, Djaem mistook Artos's eyes for twin sunrises. Still held off his feet by a powered metal arm, he watched those twin orbs burning. The screaming started, the suns closed, and Djaem was pulled closer to the man. Artos was struggling in a battle of life and death within the Ether. The howling became a lullaby as Djaem felt the rhythmic vibrations of bubbling come from inside the gauntlet that trapped him. As Artos finally fell to his knees, boiling within his own skin, Djaem was jolted just enough. A smile appeared on Djaem's face as system shock plunged him once again into blissful unconsciousness.

14

MISSION DAY TWO: WHAT THE FUCK JUST HAPPENED!

THE ETERNITY of struggle for Djaem and Scythia passed in a matter of moments for Raza and Uthraith. They ran in from the far side of the spaceport. They ran at full speed but could only watch in surprise at Djaem's bizarre initial charge and then his sacrificial second attack. Uthraith pulled Raza behind cover during Scythia's epic battle with the psychic grandmaster Artos. They felt the heat and stared in astonishment until the psychics collapsed. They approached carefully, as the deck plates were still smoldering.

Raza was silent, and Uthraith grim, as he collected his fallen companions.

"Time to go." Raza's voice sounded raw to Uthraith's ear. They ran the distance to their shuttle.

Uthraith put Djaem in the life-support medical pod. Raza hooked him in as quickly as possible. They weren't sure it would be enough to save his life. The diagnostic computer began reporting. **"Subdermal hemorrhaging, internal bleeding, extreme blood loss, concus-**

sion. . ." Raza ducked for cover as Uthraith's shot silenced the robotic voice.

"Beh shel'lah!" he growled, holstering the hand cannon. "Don't need stupid machine to tell me friend is hurt badly." He sneered at the screen. *The damn thing does no good. The only person who understood any of that is the person it is describing.* Uthraith's anger was a beast in his chest he had to wrestle down.

His fist clenched. There was nothing he could have done. The two had reached the spaceport in time to see the entire fight but were too far to help. He had seen Djaem had thrown himself into the man's leg.

They knew that the man in the armor was Artos. Uthraith was from a savage world in the far reaches of space, and even he had seen those crystals before. The crystals amplified psychic abilities. This was when he knew they were all in trouble. Scythia had muttered about the strength of the psychic needed to bind a Tyrling into their world. Someone should have warned her. Djaem should have known better. The two should not have tried to face him on their own.

They heard the snapping of Djaem's bones over his radio. They had assumed he was out cold or dead. Uthraith recognized the superior combat experience of Artos and knew that Scythia's strength alone would not be enough. Uthraith shot him with his heavy pylon rifle. It was designed to stop vehicles. Artos hadn't even noticed. Raza screamed for Scythia to run, but she had not heard.

Uthraith's anger at himself boiled in his chest. *Scythia had no fighting skills. NONE. I was so stupid to not give her even the most basic understanding of . . . Get away!* He punched the wall of the ship and dented the metal before moving out of Raza's way.

Raza's throat hurt from the screaming. Her skin was

red and stinging from the heat. She ignored it all. She didn't even scold Uthraith for his outburst. She understood his anger. It had been her job to lead the team. Her hands trembled as she finished hooking Scythia up to the other medical equipment. There was only one pod, so Scythia rested on a medical bed.

How many teams is it now? How many have I lost?

She saw Djaem charge, she saw him break, and she watched in useless rage as Artos lined Scythia up for decapitation. Raza was sure Scythia was dead.

Djaem, the cowardly rat they scraped up from some god-forsaken hive world, threw himself back into the fray. *Broken, battered, bleeding, and still he charged.* She recognized what he did, the precision of his strike. Against any other man, the fight would have ended. Djaem's blade would have pierced a lung or heart. The telekinesis allowed Artos to push against the attack. Even then Djaem still damaged him. Artos's stroke was not completely lost; with that crystal edge, the death stroke need not be lethal. Even a small wound can tear a psychic apart. His had cut deeply into Scythia's shoulder. What Raza didn't understand was what had happened next. *There was no sign of Scythia's attack.* Artos responded as if he had been hit instead.

Artos could have destroyed a strike team. If the four of them managed to stage a successful ambush, she would consider them lucky to survive. *These two idiots almost did us all in. They deserved what they got. They earned this pain.* The fear, anger, and condition of her newfound friends triggered something Uthraith had never seen. It was something Raza hadn't done in almost twenty years. Her throat clenched up as her breath hitched and tears formed in her eyes. They did not flow, but Uthraith knew they were there. They both pretended not to notice.

"Next time, just fucking let him escape!" she shouted at

the unconscious pair before she stormed off to the cockpit and made sure their automated flight plan was working.

SOON ANOTHER COMPUTER was testing Uthraith's patience. It beeped persistently and insisted that its need was urgent. Grabbing a cudgel from the wall, he stepped to answer its calls. This time, Raza was able to stop him.

Fallrick's face flickered onto the screen. "Why am I not surprised? Almost fifty guardsmen are dead. The colony is in full and open revolt and the spaceport! The fucking spaceport is STILL on fire. How! It's designed for ships' blastoffs. Raza! If anyone else answers, you take over. I need your opinion on these new guys."

"You what?" she hissed angrily as she turned to the video display. "First off, Uthraith did most of the killing of guardsmen. Secondly, the revolt was already in the works; things just got sped up a bit. And the spaceport. . . That wasn't her doing! She put the flames out, not put them there. The whole damn hive would have gone up like a fucking supernova if she hadn't stopped it. As for Djaem, anything you want to talk to me about, you can say to all of us. He's an idiot, but he's good." She was practically yelling by the end of her little speech.

They sat watching the screen for a couple minutes as the time delay caught up. Fallrick's face flashed recognition, and he offered a "Hello, Raza." Several moments later his expression changed. First annoyance, then anger, and finally shock. He closed his eyes and shook his head.

"Raza. You don't make the rules. *I* make the rules. You will play by them, or I can replace you. If you insist on doing this in front of them, so be it. You said Uthraith killed the guardsmen. I expect to see a damn good reason in your report. If the revolt was this close, why didn't I know more about it? Details! In your report. If the scum we scraped off that rock can't keep the girl under control, he's not that good. And who… exactly DID start the fire?"

Raza flinched and gathered her control after a moment. "Uh. . . well that. . . It was Djaem. He did it." She sat silently for several long minutes considering her options. She stood straight and made her decision. "But he's good. Damn good! Your new weapon didn't cause all this, but she sure as shit put an end to it. Djaem kept her calm even when she pressed beyond my ability to stay calm. We can talk about it later. Keep one of us or replace all four. It's your choice. But good luck finding any team that could have handled what went down in that burning hell. I ain't waiting through this space lag to give my report. You want to know what happened, then send the coordinates. We'll figure it out from there." She disconnected the communications link. After a few minutes, coordinates were sent. The shuttle flew on.

SCYTHIA REGAINED HER SENSES. Pain, the old companion, had returned. There was a dull throbbing pains and sharp stabs. Her whole body felt heavy; every scrape and bruise, fresh and aching. She was completely in the now, and the flesh. She strained, trying to reach the Ether, but it was a faraway voice, a whisper in the background of the world. She had a moment of panic until she touched it, felt the embers there. Fuel was spent but the fire remained.

Djaem! Without her power, she had to search with only her eyes. A cry of pain escaped as she forced herself to sit upright. Clear tears ran from her eyes as she moved, slowly and agonizingly, closer to the med-pod. She finally made the chair positioned next to it. Pressing her face against the glass of the pod, she looked in at Djaem sleeping.

"He's a fucking idiot," Raza's voice came closer. "What handler risks their life to save their asset?" She shook her head. "And you seemed out of it. You alright?"

Scythia was tired. It took effort to make her voice work. "My power. . . I used up all my fire." She rested her cheek against the glass to look at Raza. "Thank you for saving us," she said in a small voice. She continued watching the rise and fall of Djaem's chest.

Raza watched the Star-born carefully. "What did you do to him?" her voice low, almost menacing. "You brainwashed him? Mind control?" She looked at Djaem and then back at Scythia's face. "He is a con and a coward. The man has the sex drive of a eunuch: I know you aren't having sex. How did you get him to risk himself like that? Not once, but twice."

Scythia was confused by the question, but she answered, "I gave him my trust. He said that was what he wanted," Raza's mouth fell open in surprise. Her eyes widened with disbelief and frustration.

The machines continued beeping.

Scythia finally said in a worried voice, "Did he always look like this?" His face was swollen and discolored.

Raza sighed and rubbed her neck. "No. He's torn up bad, inside and out. Djaem ain't a fighter. He runs and hides, gets others to fight. And this is why!" Raza shifted from her usual angry tone to a softer one, concern written on her face. "If we don't get him to a big ship. . . he's not pulling this one out. If he survives, he'll be messed up forever."

Blue hands clenched. Scythia felt the twist of helplessness. She could use the Ether to cause mass destruction but could not fix anything? *I failed. I was supposed to protect him.*

Without the Ether to distract her, she was fully aware of her surroundings. She heard everything Raza was saying. Scythia turned towards the woman, finally giving her full attention. Surprise took over Scythia's expression. She hadn't realized how pretty Raza was. Everyone looked so different outside of the Ether.

"Forever?" she whispered, sadness settling heavily in her chest. It was so hard to speak, and her mind was fogged with pain. She swallowed as fear settled somewhere in her stomach. She might lose him. If Djaem died, he would become like the ashes of her memory. His music would end. She didn't want to be alone in the darkness of the world. She wanted his light.

"Yes, He was down on the first hit. He should have stayed down. When you cut up your insides, it can mess you up forever. So, I need to know. . . Did you do something? Why did he do it? Why'd he get back up?"

"I don't know. His thoughts burn bright in the Ether, but I was blinded by fire. The Ether was a hurricane." Scythia voice quaked as she tried to explain. "I was deaf, I only knew he was hurt because of our link."

Her breath hitched as lightening shot down her side. Pain in the Here was so different from in the Ether. "I was supposed to protect him." Her voice broke as she spoke. Tears now slid down her cheeks.

"In the fight with Artos, you used more power than ever before. Why'd you do that? The mission?" Raza prodded, probing not only for answers but reactions.

Scythia tried find a way to explain. "What mission? There was no mission. . . just me and him. . . his will against mine. He wanted to end me, so I needed to end him." She wiped tears from her face. "While I was containing the fire in the spaceport, I learned. Ether is everywhere, inside all of us." A blue hand rested on her chest. "We all have a candle inside of us. Me, you, Djaem, even Uthraith. It is the light of our souls. I ignited his very essence and then poured all my fuel into him. It burned his candle to ash." She looked back at Djaem. Her face took on a blank expression. "Soul fire is what was used to burn me out of my own mind."

Raza kept her expression blank as she tried to figure out if there was a veiled threat. Assessing Scythia, she decided there was not. Raza was surprised at the difference in Scythia.

Scythia's words poured out clear and free of the Ether. "The breaker used his soul fire to ignite my memories, burning away what made me. . . me. I tricked him and ignited us both. We burned together. My will is forged out of that fire. Everyone has one, a flame that lights their way in the darkness of the Ether. Djaem has prisms that encircle his light. One light reflected and amplified by the crystals of his mind." She looked at Raza. "He is special." Scythia's normal black pupils looked strange in the light of the med bay. They were a swirl of red and blue. As if someone tried to make purple but had only half stirred. Raza realized it was the Ether that gave her eyes that empty black color. Those eye pierced Raza with an intense expression; it left her shaken and unnerved. "We all have fires, which means we all have fuel. . ." Scythia's mind began to form an answer. Raza was not certain she wanted to know what the question had been. "Tell me. . . what is wrong with Djaem?" Scythia's voice took on the hard edge of conviction.

Raza covered her agitation with feigned annoyance. "His broken bones are out of place; one of them is pressing into his diaphragm. He's bleeding inside; the med-pod has to drain it out and put it back in where it belongs. And he has a bruise on his brain."

Scythia nodded. "Artos could move things with the Ether. When his light started to fade, I pushed on it to keep it there. I believe I can do the same thing for Djaem. I just need fuel for my power."

Raza decided to focus on the positive in that statement. "Psychic surgery? That'd be great, if you were su—"

A clicking sound came from the med-pod. Warnings flashed on the remaining screens. The diagnostic board scrambled to keep up. "**Increased hemorrhaging, extreme internal temperature with suspected foreign body, internal cauterization**." Over the course of a few minutes, the alarms quieted, and the list of injuries reduced to something manageable.

Scythia wavered, bracing with her good hand on the glass of the pod. Slowly she slid to the floor. *So tired*. Her own wound seeped red through her bandages.

Raza fell to Scythia's power a second time. First, to her knees, then fully onto the floor. She was overcome by a sense of intense hunger, fear, and intrusion. Her limbs no longer responded. They were trembling meat bags attached to her torso. Her voice failed her. Only her face told of the horror she was experiencing. She was helpless, a worm on the hook trying to avoid the water.

Scythia crawled over to Raza. She gently petted Raza's head with her good hand. Pulling out a small hard candy she put it in Raza's mouth. Scythia awkwardly helped Raza sit propped up against the wall. There the two women rested, exhausted.

"Thank you," Scythia said in a small, sad voice. "I only took a tiny bit. Just enough of your fuel to help him. You will be alright. It will pass, your fire is strong. The sugar helps." She smiled at a job well done. "I don't know what happens if I take too much. Not yet anyway. That was about as much energy I use when I don't push. I am glad. I was worried it wouldn't be enough. Thank you. I am so tired now." Scythia's head fell on Raza's shoulder, asleep.

RAZA WAS HELPLESSLY PROPPED and utterly terrified. Scythia had learned a valuable and deadly lesson from Raza. People can be tools. Raza understood that it was her own fault. Now she had an idea of the power this monster had. Scythia was learning, building new abilities. Just like a child, she observed and makes it real. Raza realized that Scythia's whim contained more power than Raza had in her entire being.

Wake up, Djaem! Your monster needs you!

THE PAIN FADED ABRUPTLY. The bliss of sweet nothings had embraced Djaem. *Oh, thank you, old ones, I am dead. Finally.* This mission had not been for a first-time recruit. He was certain it was his death sentence, and it had been achieved.

The warmth of his blanket of darkness was not perfect. It burned at times. Even unconscious, he realized this was bad. It meant he was dying, not yet dead. He wasn't worried. Just a little longer and he would be there. He heard the song of the angels. He saw the faint light growing brighter as he pushed his mind towards it. Soon, all pain would be gone. There would be no more struggle, no more strife. He could have peace.

As the light expanded and brightened, one of the angels spoke to him. He could not understand the words.

He tried to respond but found only gibberish in his mouth. The angel spoke again.

"You're such an idiot!"

These were not the words he expected of an angel. He blinked against the light and tried to clear the fog from his mind. It would not budge, but the pain returned. "What?"

Raza repeated herself. "You. . . are. . . a. . . fucking. . . idiot."

Djaem tried to sit up to look at her. Agony shot through him, telling him that she was indeed correct, and he was a fucking idiot. "We've got to work on your communication skills. What's the problem now?" He managed to get his retort out through gritted teeth.

"For one," Raza began in a serious tone, "reign your fucking monster in! She's beyond out of control. Second, you're a fucking moron. Never try to take down someone like that by yourself. And third, you're a world class fucking idiot. I saw you."

Djaem laughed but pain turned it into coughing. Raza smiled. Both the laughing and the pain that followed had been her goal.

"You damn near got yourself killed, and that could have gotten all of us dusted."

Djaem lowered his gaze. "I just. . . I was trying. . . Listen, I messed up. I missed what Artos was really doing."

"Oh, shut up!" Raza snapped, actually angry this time. "Everyone makes mistakes, especially in this job. I couldn't care less about you not seeing Artos was involved. We all missed that. That's not even close to the problem. Seriously, though, what kind of handler moves in to try to physically assault the beast who just took on their own beast?"

Djaem was confused, thinking she meant the robed

man from the cavern. That was what that cultist fool had done. "What? Him? Yeah, that's why I—"

"IDIOT! I mean you! Scythia is your weapon, your beast, your monster. You're her handler. She fights, not you. You think you can save her by sacrificing yourself. You get yourself killed, and she's done. They will end her. Or more accurately they'll try to put her down. And that is a whole other mess. Her life can protect yours. It doesn't work the other way around. Uthraith is my meat shield. It doesn't work if I try to fight his battles for him." She huffed in frustration.

Djaem realized what he had done. *What WAS I thinking?* He rolled the start of the situation over in his mind, looking for an answer. His near-perfect memory must have been affected by his concussion. Scythia being in danger was all he could remember thinking about when Artos appeared in the flames.

"He saw all our faces; he talked to me. A psychic that powerful can trac—"

"Bullshit! Tell your lies to someone who might believe them. Try again."

"She was the only weapon we had with any chance of stopping him! He was in the spaceport. We had no other way out!" Djaem pushed himself to a slightly propped position, and anger was clear in his voice. Inside, he knew. *This anger is not for Raza.* He continued to try to find his thoughts and reasons for his actions. He continued to come up blank.

"Better. Better. That one almost makes sense. If he killed her, he would take our shuttle and leave, no problem for us. . . Noth—"

"No! I can't just let him kill her! Arghh. . ." The concussion started pushing on Djaem's head from the inside. It felt like an overinflated balloon shortly before it popped.

"There it is," Raza said in a calm and pleasant voice. "The truth. You think about it, Djaem. Never put my life in the bag when you take a gamble like that again. You're such a fucking idiot." She sighed and took pity on the idiot. She could tell him the rest later. She didn't say anything as she walked away.

15

RETURN TRIP DAY TWO, YEAH. . . BUT DID YOU DIE?

SCYTHIA DREAMED. For the first time in memory, the Ether didn't have her sleeping mind. Her subconscious was free of its influence. She dreamed of things she had no name for. She dreamed of drowning, of fire, of pain, and then of Djaem. He reached out of the black, pulling her out of the burning liquid. Once he pulled her free, she fell upward and landed on something soft, floating on cool clouds. Her hands searched for Djaem, but he was gone. She rolled and moved, trying to find him in the clouds. Fear gripped her heart as she called his name.

In a panic, she feared he was gone forever.

Scythia jerked awake, pain searing down her side from her wounded shoulder. Her eyes looked around, trying to orientate herself in the real world. Being only in the phys-ical world left her disjointed. She was lying on the medical bay's second bed. Slowly she rolled her head to one side. Relief filled her as she saw Djaem propped up, sipping water. His wounds, no longer life threatening, were progressing quickly. Her body relaxed and her breathing became easier.

Her embers were beginning to rekindle. The Ether was slowly growing louder. It remained distant but more distinct. She blinked and tried to decide if she wanted to move or if lying there was a better idea. The pain from her shoulder only seemed to grow. She kept her body still while she watched Djaem. She knew her recovery was going to be a slow and tedious process. But she was content as long as Djaem was there.

DJAEM KNEW the moment she gasped awake. He had been listening since her nightmare began. It was the first time she ever had one. *Why is she having nightmares now? Why not after her breaking?* He had whispered and she had calmed. Now he felt the weight of her gaze. It was comforting and familiar. She smiled when their eyes met. Her face was swollen on one side. Her arm was strapped to her chest. She was covered in wrapped bandages from the waist up. The white was a stark contrast against her blue skin. He smiled inwardly.

It is strange to see her blood. She should bleed fire, or mist.

Her voice was a hoarse whisper, like the air hurt to pass from her mouth. "You got hurt, I failed." Tears welled in her eyes threatening to spill down her cheeks "It won't happen again. I'll do better. . . please. Don't go."

He frowned at the break in her voice. Her eyes were a swirling pattern of red, blue, and that impossible black. He could see the fear in them. Like a child afraid of being left behind. He tried hard to ignore the clenched fist in his chest.

He made sure his voice was steady and gave her a small smile. "We both failed. I made mistakes too. We will both do better. Don't worry, I am not leaving," he said, trying to put her worries to rest. Even he was surprised at the certainty he heard there.

She smiled, her face relaxing, and her eyes closing for a moment. It was just the span of a few heartbeats before she was watching him again. Her fear was gone, but the concern remained.

"Are you feeling better?" She fought against her eyes drifting shut again.

Djaem smiled and used a soothing tone to help her lose that fight. "Yes. I will be fine soon. Rest. You need it."

She forced her eyes wide again. "Djaem? Raza said you made a mistake. You are saying you made a mistake. What did you do that was so bad?" She forced herself to shift upward. She groaned as she propped herself up. The pain helped her remain awake.

Is she afraid to sleep? Djaem pondered that while he considered how to answer.

"I. . . I'm not supposed to be in the heavy fights. Compared to others, I'm slow, weak, and frail. Jumping into the fight alone was extremely dumb," he said mostly to himself.

"Why did you?" She waited while Djaem sighed and stammered, looking for a reason he could explain. When he failed, she smiled softly.

"It wasn't a mistake," she said firmly. "You did what you always do. You protected me. You promised to take care of me if I trusted you. That's what you did. I will be more careful to keep you safe next time."

Djaem smiled and gave a small, nervous laugh. "True. But that's not how I'm supposed to do it. Honestly, my biggest mistake was missing the threat to start with." He gave her a big smile. "You did amazing; don't worry. You did perfectly fine. I made my share of mistakes and I learned from them. Now rest."

Scythia quirked her head but finally lowered herself back down. "Was one of the mistakes going into the wide open? I know how hard that must have been for you."

Djaem flushed in embarrassment. "What, no! I wasn't thinking about the open space, I was just waiting for the others." He tried to ignore that shame and confusion those moments crated.

"Were you thinking about me? Worrying?" Her head cocked to the other side, much like an animal hearing a distant and unfamiliar sound.

"I. . . what? No. I mean of course I was worried." Djaem tripped over his answers. "About you and what might happen if Artos escaped. He is a dangerous man. He had influence and power. He would have become a big problem for us," he said, trying to brush off the awkwardness.

You used to be such a better liar. His mind mocked him. *Shut up, it's fine. She is medicated and will barely remember what I said,* he replied with confidence. The inner voice whispered in malicious victory. *So, you admit that was a lie? But the truth is… SHUTUP!* He silenced his inner voice before it had a thought he couldn't come back from.

Scythia nodded. "Yes. . . he is. . ."

"Was," Djaem corrected automatically and then froze. His face blanched as fearful nausea rolled in his belly. "We. . . you made sure he couldn't. . . hurt anymore people." By the time he finished speaking, Djaem was trembling.

"No." Scythia's voice was small in the med bay. "You said it right the first time. You felt it too. I still feel it. He is a dangerous man. He has ties to the Ether. He's not gone. . . not yet, but I am stronger in the Ether."

"What? No. . . How? I saw. . . I saw what you did. There's no way. . ." Djaem started to dry-heave with disgust and panic. Scythia slowly rose and limped over to Djaem's bed. Softly she placed a hand on his shoulder.

"He's in the Ether now. He is trapped. He can't reach you. You are okay." She tried to sound reassuring.

"Yeah. . . yeah. . . I just . . . That was . . ."

"I understand," Scythia interrupted, stopping his line of thinking. She brushed hair from his face. "I see things like that ever since I first started remembering. This was your first one, wasn't it?"

Djaem nodded, fighting his instinctual reaction to grab her and curl into a ball.

"Then we shouldn't talk about it!" she said with cheerful finality. She gingerly sat on the bed beside him. "When we get to the next planet, can we practice table manners again? I enjoyed that. I also want to listen to music. There were only a few little samples on the data crystals."

A pep and energy entered her voice. Her smile was gentle but bright. She had learned enough from Raza and Djaem to understand that a change in conversation was needed. Djaem found himself joining in the smile.

They talked about the last time they practiced table manners. He smiled and teased her a bit about her mistakes. The idle chitchat helped replace the horrible memories in his mind with happier thoughts.

She gasped suddenly; her eyes wide as she looked around urgently. He froze. "WHAT?"

She pouted and looked at him with big sad eyes. "I lost my shoes!" Big tears filled her eyes. He blinked and smiled as he tried not to laugh. She wiped her eyes. "Oh, Gem. . . I am sorry. . ."

He reached out and petted her head. "It's okay, dearest. . . I will get you a new pair. Don't cry. We will go together, and you can pick them out."

She sniffled and looked up in delight. "We can?"

He smiled and nodded. "Of course." He again ignored the squeezing sensation in his chest as she beamed at him. *It is just the injuries recovering. That's all it is. . . right?*

"Thank you," she said and carefully curled up around him on the small bed. He petted her orange flame hair as she fell asleep.

16

NO, YOU DIDN'T DIE

IT TOOK them three days to reach the coordinates sent by Fallrick. Both Scythia and Djaem were on bed rest and pain meds for the duration of the trip, so they spent most of the time sleeping. Scythia's energy had returned quickly, and she was able to heal her wound, leaving a long, jagged scar. Uthraith told her a scar was a symbol of pride. It was proof of her survival. She smiled and nodded, "It is a physical memory. This cannot be taken from me. Even if the memory is gone, the scar will remain." She smiled any time she looked at it.

Uthraith spent time cleaning and carving her demon skull. He blackened the bone, staining it with deep blues and filled the etching with melted copper. The careful etching and grooves created an elaborate and delicate pattern. Copper flowers blended into swirls of smoke and ancient glyphs of power. It glittered and shined on black-blue bone. For Djaem he crafted a small, curved blade, easily concealable. It was designed to be held underhanded and spin. The razor edge and feather light material made it sing through the air as it spun. However, the edge was so hard it could cut through almost anything. The time he spent crafting he considered how his companions had come so close to death. He would not allow this to happen a second time.

Djaem was mostly recovered the day of arrival. He had dreamed of twin sunrises every night. He was much less troubled by the vastness of space, but more so by his dreams. Scythia was much more talkative this trip. She said she was drained. He wasn't sure why, but it helped keep her from becoming so lost in the Ether. Djaem found when she was alert and attentive, she was clever and funny. The ship was full of Uthraith's laughter. She was becoming quite good at the card games Raza was teaching her. Djaem was teaching her how to cheat. For three days they traveled through the stars, safe in their like pocket of artificial air. Djaem could see the bonds forming strengthen.

Raza gave them strict instructions when it was time to disembark. Fallrick communicated directly with her. She was the team leader. Djaem was completely content to have her remain so. Scythia didn't bat an eye as she gathered up her belongings. It never occurred to her to question the where, or why. She lacked any training or experience in long-term thinking. *I must find a way to help her with that.* Djaem didn't want her to fall into traps when he wasn't around. Uthraith was simply used to not knowing and didn't care. Djaem, as per usual, took note.

RAZA DID her best to prepare herself. *First, our debriefing with Fallrick. This isn't going to go well.* She had carefully instructed each of her team, coaching them on the story of what had happened at the hive colony. Scythia was under strict orders of how she was to behave and conduct herself.

Even Uthraith was given a careful script he was either to follow or say nothing. She knew Djaem would be able to handle himself, she just hoped that he would.

The coordinates were a spot of empty space six days from the Citadel planet. Waiting in that spot was Fallrick's personal transport ship. The shuttle docked with the transport. Fallrick's transport was tiny compared to the massive transport they had taken to get to the hive mine but was capable of Ether-space travel. The solar sails were open, shimmering in gold as they recharged. As they stepped off the shuttle, they all saw the crystals embedded in the plating. Raza frowned and couldn't remember seeing them there before. *Those look just like the crystals Artos was taking. They are new, and expensive. He is taking precautions.*

SCYTHIA GASPED and stumbled as she exited the shuttle. Her hand went to her mouth as she had a heavy wave of nausea. Djaem took her arm, and Uthraith asked, "You, okay Little Blue?" Scythia simply nodded and braced herself for boarding. She did not like this place. *It's so empty.*

Once inside the ship, there was no Ether. She whispered into Djaem's ear, "The Ether was left outside."

Fallrick met them in person just inside the airlock. He did not look pleased. He pointed to the row of seats that lined one wall. "Everyone but you," he said, glaring at Raza, "sit! You, with me!"

Djaem patted Raza's back in assurance and quietly went to the seats, helping Scythia along. Uthraith nodded to Raza and took a seat. Scythia started humming her little tune, but the tone was of desperation. After the door behind Raza and Fallrick sealed and the sound dampeners were engaged, Djaem took out the audio device that connected to the listening bug he had just placed on **Raza's** back. They didn't have a visual, but they could hear everything just fine.

"What the hell is wrong with you? I gave you the most powerful weapons I could find, and you used them with such reckless disregard? Do you even remember your orders? Your place?" There was a pause, and Fallrick spoke again. "You should show it! That tone, on the radio. Unacceptable. You do not talk to me like that. I lead, you follow. This is the only way this is going to work. Or would you rather be back on Rythis?"

They could hear her gasp, but she didn't speak. Rythis was one of the dark points in the Empire's history that for some reason just never cleared itself up. It started as a prison world, but then valuable minerals were discovered there. Instead of moving the prisoners and letting corporations move in, the corporations were allowed to take over security responsibilities in exchange for harvesting rights. The prisoners were then used as slave labor. It was as bad as it was imagined to be. Two tidbits made this worse. First, new prisoners were still delivered to corporations based on their promises of production. Second, those born there were kept there. While they were not prisoners, they could not afford to leave and were put to work in exchange for food, shelter, and water by the corporations.

Djaem knew Raza was not born on Rythis, but it seemed somehow, she ended up there. She would do anything to keep from going back. *Anyone in their right mind would never want to go there, but she had firsthand knowledge and knew it was worse than most believe.* Djaem pondered this for a moment. This was tremendous motivation but was not the root of her loyalty to Fallrick.

A flapping sound came across the listening device as a stack of thick papers was thrown onto a desk. A few moments later, Raza spoke. "He didn't really kill that many people. And he can be hard to control." Uthraith looked at the other two and shook his head. Flipping sounds came over the device. "That. . . is a lot of damage," Raza continued.

"If you can't control him, someone else will. . . or he has to go. I mean die. Would that be easier?" Fallrick's voice sounded frustrated and fed up. Uthraith's face shifted into a defiant, angry grimace.

"I can. I will. This won't happen again."

"You allowed your weapon to unleash this kind of devastation! This will come back on me, you know. Look at this. Walls in the tunnels are melted! MELTED. An inspector —a HIGHER RANKING inspector—is now dead. I'm trusting you with the power of this weapon. Did I overestimate you? You've never let me down before."

"Hey," Raza rebutted, "it was our first time out. Artos was tied into the Ether-ling presence and the crystals and the kidnappings. And look at this. See? Your 'weapon' could have done much worse. It may not have been perfect, but this was far from out of control."

Scythia lowered her head and muttered, "Did I make trouble for her?"

Djaem shook his head. "No. . . I don't think so."

There had been a long period on the listener. Only heavy sighs and the flipping of papers could be heard. Fallrick finally spoke, "You have the most dangerous person in the sector under your charge. You have the power to destroy entire colonies. You need to step up your game. Reign Djaem in. You will have to go before a review. I will mitigate the damage as much as possible. You have to be more careful in the future or I won't be able to protect any of you."

Djaem simply nodded. *I'm 'the' weapon. . . I'm Scythia's*

handler, but Raza is mine. A weapon! This guy thinks I'm more dangerous than his psychic bomb over here. I'm the weapon. . . alright, then. . . safety's off.

To everyone's surprise, the two started talking in lighter tones, on lighter topics. Family, mutual friends, and personal activities all came up.

BEING CUT off from the Ether, Scythia had trouble relaxing at first. Eventually, however, she came to rest against Djaem. Shifting so that she could put her head in his lap, she looked up at him. Once again, she was fascinated by Djaem's face. The general neutrality of his features. She kept forgetting that his face looks so different than his mind. He was neither tall like Uthraith nor short like Raza. He was neither skinny nor fat, just an average lean like that of a runner. His face gave nothing away about ethnicity. He was deeply tan, but that could be from hundreds of worlds. He was neither handsome nor ugly. Taken individually, each part of his face was average: a normal-looking nose, a firm but pleasant mouth, an average pair of nut-brown eyes. His hair was a dark brown with just enough wave to not be straight. It was a little longer than when they had first met. Added together, he was perfectly plain. Like he was the absolute neutral. If she closed her eyes to picture his face, what she pictured was always wrong.

She had stopped listening to the conversation and played a little game with herself. She smiled as she looked up at Djaem's face, closing her eyes and then peeling them open again slowly, each time amazed. Each time she had pictured him wrong. Either too handsome or too ugly.

DJAEM TOLERATED her weird grinning stare with the same patience he tolerated most of her behavior. She was still and relaxed—that was all he needed. *Besides only the ancient ones know what she was actually seeing?* He shifted her so that she rested more easily on his thigh, his attention still on the listening device. His mind whirled and weaved his plans as his idle fingers combed gently through her flaming hair. It was soft and silky as it glided easily between his fingers. He used her far shoulder as an armrest, bracing his wrist there as he focused inwardly. Completely unaware of what his hand was doing, the physical contact once again unnaturally natural for him.

UTHRAITH WATCHED them for a moment before he shook his head. They seemed incredibly fragile. While they ignored him, he pondered the unusual pair. *She is one of those dolls of blown glass: All stretched and elongated form, and coloring, bright and shiny. He is a toy made of sticks, brown and rough edges. But for all her shine, she was transparent. For all his plainness, he had everything hidden beneath.*

He considered the oddity of this group. All opposite forces tipping back and forth wildly. They were all dangerous in their own way. All monsters in the extremity of their skill. *Will we tear each other to bits or find the strength to pull each other into balance?* He was concerned. It would be very hard for him to take the Star-born. She could break him with her mind in less than a heartbeat. *I am not sure I could take her by surprise. Djaem would see it coming.* He smiled to himself and relaxed against the wall, tilting his head back and closing his eyes. *This was better. It will force Raza to know her limits and force her to trust.* Having satisfied his thoughts, he fell asleep.

WITHOUT THE NOISE of the Ether, Scythia's mind was clear, and it was easier to consider the possibilities. In the silence of her head, Scythia tried to mirror Djaem's behavior. She tried to figure out what steps she needed to take. Everyone believed her mind weak. That she was like a child or that she was mad. They thought of her as less. *That is good. Let them think so.* She would not let Fallrick hurt her friends. She was more than the Ether. She could be more than a weapon.

Djaem was focused on eavesdropping. Scythia relaxed as he stroked her hair gently. The sound of his heartbeat and breathing filled the vacancy left by the Ether. She curled around his warmth and let the rhythm of his breathing send her off to sleep.

Isolated from the Ether, her dreams were like that of a child, unformed and unhindered. She dreamed of music she didn't know, of lights illuminating spaceship corridors she had never walked in. She dreamed of laughter and warmth. She saw starlight and nebulas floating in the vastness of space. Her mind was free of fears and regrets. This was where the last bits of herself had been hidden. That was how she had defeated the invader that had burned so much of her away. This was her refuge. Here, kept deep in the stars of her subconscious, was her unbreakable will. She would fill the empty space with new memories.

Stars are born from the dust and gas of a nebula. Scythia knew she was the same. She was a star born from the ashes of her memory, burning bright in the dark oceans of the universe.

AFTERWORD

Thank you so much for joining me on this adventure. Please be sure to subscribe to my newsletter and get notifications on the next book.

ALSO BY JESSE M. HARVEY

Science Fiction/Apocalypse Survival/Adventure:
Motherhood at the End of the World

ABOUT THE AUTHOR

Jesse M. Harvey is a thirty-nine-year-old mother of three. She is originally from El Paso, Texas, and spent many years in southern California.

She now lives in an alien landscape called Central New York. Having spent years of her childhood as a military brat, she felt it only proper to marry a man who would understand all her jokes, so she chose a Navy veteran.

www.ingramcontent.com/pod-product-compliance
Lightning Source LLC
Chambersburg PA
CBHW030752200726
48288CB00004B/1145